V.G. 7/06
F.N.E.

W9-AUK-376

A movement from across the street caught his attention through the window.

The pencil Holt Tanner was holding snapped in two as he watched Molly Brewster skip up the front steps of the library.

She wore a white dress with no sleeves, and as she moved, the waves of her hair—not tied up in a knot today for once—drifted around her bare shoulders.

Then, in one moment before she disappeared inside, she looked across the wide street, almost as if she sensed his attention. And maybe she could see Holt sitting there, behind the half-opened blinds of his window, for she suddenly turned and darted inside the library as if the devil himself was after her.

She was bold and saucy one minute. Nervous and skittish the next.

Holt shoved away from his desk, stuffing his little notepad in his pocket. "I'll be at the library," he told his dispatcher.

"You might consider wiping the drool off your chin before you go over there," his dispatcher replied.

Allison Leigh
Montana Lawman

Silhouette Books

Published by Silhouette Books
America's Publisher of Contemporary Romance

If you purchased this book without a cover you should be aware that this book is stolen property. It was reported as "unsold and destroyed" to the publisher, and neither the author nor the publisher has received any payment for this "stripped book."

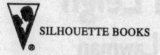

SILHOUETTE BOOKS

ISBN 0-373-36029-0

MONTANA LAWMAN

Copyright © 2002 by Harlequin Books S.A.

All rights reserved. Except for use in any review, the reproduction or utilization of this work in whole or in part in any form by any electronic, mechanical or other means, now known or hereafter invented, including xerography, photocopying and recording, or in any information storage or retrieval system, is forbidden without the written permission of the publisher, Silhouette Books, 233 Broadway, New York, NY 10279 U.S.A.

All characters in this book have no existence outside the imagination of the author and have no relation whatsoever to anyone bearing the same name or names. They are not even distantly inspired by any individual known or unknown to the author, and all incidents are pure invention.

This edition published by arrangement with Harlequin Books S.A.

® and TM are trademarks of the publisher. Trademarks indicated with ® are registered in the United States Patent and Trademark Office, the Canadian Trade Marks Office and in other countries.

Visit Silhouette Books at www.eHarlequin.com

Printed in U.S.A.

The knocking grew to a thunderous sound.

The door. Someone was at the door. Pounding louder than her heartbeat, making the door shudder nearly as much as she was.

Shaking her head at her foolishness, Molly pushed off the couch and hurriedly crossed the living room toward the door. The nightmare she'd been having clung to her mind, making her feel more fuzzy than ever, and her hand shook as she grabbed hold of the doorknob.

She no longer lived in fear.

She deliberately yanked open the door, if only to prove to herself that the nightmare was nothing but imaginings. The tall man standing on the other side, though, nearly startled her right out of the few wits she still possessed. Her hand kept a tight, sweaty hold of the doorknob.

Control. She scrambled frantically for the mantra. *You are in control.*

She made herself look at him, gaze skimming up the blue jeans, stuttering over the badge hooked over his belt, traveling over a hard torso clad in a khaki-colored uniform shirt that was probably crisp when he'd put it on, but now looked more than a little wilted because of the heat. Beyond that, to his sharp features, black hair and dark, inscrutable brown eyes, she couldn't force herself to look. Control only went so far, and the man had made her feel itchy from the first time she'd seen him, even before she'd known *what* he was.

The doorknob was practically making a permanent imprint on the palm of her hand, but she still couldn't seem to make herself let go. "Deputy Tanner. What are you d-doing here?"

Special thanks and acknowledgment are given to Allison Leigh for her contribution to the MONTANA MAVERICKS series.

For my girls

Holt Tanner slid his dark glasses down a notch, eyeing the woman clinging to her door as if it were a life raft. Approximate height, five-five. Weight about one-fifteen. Age had been listed as twenty-seven, but she looked even younger...regardless, she was too damned young for him.

Annoyed with the thought, Holt pulled off his sunglasses completely and tucked them in his shirt. "I need to ask you some questions, Ms. Brewster."

There wasn't one lick of color in her alabaster face. If anything, she looked as if she'd seen a ghost. As they had almost from the moment he'd met Molly Brewster when he'd first moved to Rumor eight months ago, her eyes glanced at him, then away. Just long enough for him to get a gut-tightening sight of those incredibly light-blue eyes surrounded by lush black lashes. Just long enough for him to wonder, yet again, what she was hiding.

If there was one thing Deputy Sheriff Holt Tanner knew for certain, it was that he couldn't afford to trust Molly Brewster. She was secretive, for one thing. And she made him hot, for another. One or the other irritation was bad enough, but the combination of the two was definitely no good for his peace of mind.

To be clichéd about it—been there, done that.

"Regarding?" Her delicate brows arched in query, and the coolness of her voice was completely belied by the fact that she looked as if a sharp word would make her shatter.

"Harriet Martel's death."

"I answered all of your questions at the sheriff station weeks ago."

He looked past her into the dim coolness of her

living room, noticing the way she shifted when he did so. As if she didn't want him to see inside. Considering he was a good half foot taller than she was, she could shift all she wanted and he'd still see over her head into the pin-neat home.

There was a flowered couch, an armchair, a coffee table with a book on it, and little else to indicate the type of person dwelling there. "You were very cooperative when you came to the station," he agreed smoothly. "And you've been cooperative since then when we've spoken. May I come in?"

Her lips were pale, vulnerably nude and soft looking until they drew up all tight the way they invariably did whenever he was around her. "It's a, um, a terrible mess."

He considered telling her that she should never bother lying. She was pretty miserable at it. But he was used to people who didn't want to talk with a cop no matter what the circumstances. She just didn't know that he wasn't one to give up on a case.

No matter what the cost.

"We could always talk down at the station," he said pointedly. "One way or the other, Ms. Brewster, I do intend to talk with you."

Her lashes swept down, and it looked to him as if she was conducting a mental struggle. "Have a seat," she said after a moment, "and I'll bring out some cold lemonade."

The concession was better than nothing. But he made no move toward the two iron chairs sitting on her railed porch until she'd carefully closed the front door in his face.

Whistling tunelessly, Holt dropped down onto one of the chairs—the one closest to the front door. He tugged loose the top button on his shirt and dragged the brown tie even looser. Who'd have thought he'd have to leave a lifetime in L.A. for a dinky town in Montana to find out just how miserable August heat could be?

He stretched his legs out in front of him and studied the quiet street on which Molly Brewster, librarian, lived. The town park was only a block away, and in the silent afternoon he could hear the occasional shriek or laugh coming from that direction.

He could feel the minutes ticking by as surely as he could feel the sweat creeping down his neck. He twitched his tie again, stretched out his legs a little more and watched an ugly little spider creep across the whitewashed eave. It, at least, seemed oblivious to the heat that had been making even the most even-keeled people in town cranky.

The creak of the door warned him the moment before Molly stepped out onto the porch, carrying two tall, slender glasses. Lemon slices and ice cubes jostled as she carefully stepped past him to set one of the glasses on the small table separating the chairs. Without looking at him, she sat down, cradling her own glass in both hands.

He looked at her. Feet encased in tidy white tennis shoes placed squarely on the wooden porch; the hem of her lightweight blue sundress tugged down as near to her knees as possible.

Shapely knees.

He stifled a sigh and picked up his glass of lemonade. It was tart and refreshing and he barely kept from guzzling it down because of the damned afternoon heat. Because her knees were smooth and way too beckoning. Because she was a decade younger than he was, and he wasn't there to notice her damned, pretty knees.

He set the lemonade back on the glass-and-iron table with a tad more force than was wise, and was grateful the glass didn't just crack right then and there. "You found the body a little more than four weeks ago."

She was staring fixedly ahead of her, but at least there was more color in her face, so he wasn't concerned she might keel over in a dead faint.

"I found *Harriet,* Deputy." Her voice was soft, but held a distinct edge.

"You were friends with her."

"Most people called her the head librarian, considering the small staff we have, but she was actually the director of the public library. My boss," Molly corrected. "As you well know. She reported directly to the board of trustees for the library."

"And now you're the head librarian."

At that, she seemed to sigh a little. "The library needs to have someone in charge. Rather like the sheriff department, I should think."

He watched her thumb glide back and forth over the moisture condensing on her glass. Her nails were unpainted, neatly groomed, cut short. If she was the type to chew her nails, she hid it well.

His ex-wife had spent a weekly fortune having her nails kept long and viper red. He watched Molly's thumb a moment longer. Her unvarnished, natural-looking fingers were a far cry more feminine than Vanessa's could ever claim to have been. The thought snuck in, out of place and definitely unwanted.

"Why is it that Sheriff Reingard assigned Harriet's case to you, anyway?"

It was a fair enough question, though he could have done without the challenging attitude underlying her words. "I was a detective in California before I came to Montana."

Her expression didn't change. "What was your crime that you were banished all the way from sunny California to our little town?"

"You think Rumor is a destination for those who are banished? Is that why *you're* here from… wherever?"

"Sunday afternoons are generally spent with family and friends around here," she said after a moment, not addressing his question any more than he'd addressed hers. "At the Calico Diner or the Rooftop Café."

"Pretty hot afternoon to spend at the Rooftop unless you can get a seat inside." He picked up his glass and drank down another third. But she was right. Rumor was the kind of place where families spent Sunday afternoons together. They had dinner together either at home or at one of the popular places in town, or they had picnics down at the park.

They weren't sitting on the porches of librarians conducting a murder investigation. That was definitely more *Holt's* type of life. Even Dave Reingard was probably bellying up to a pot roast and garden salad with his wife Dee Dee and their five kids.

"Yet, fortunately for me, you're home on a Sunday afternoon," he said blandly. "Family and friends give you the day off today or something?"

Her lips tightened a little and he nearly smiled. He knew for a fact that Ms. Molly Brewster was as standoffish as he was. Maybe more. Yet she'd worked with Harriet Martel as the assistant librarian for all of the eighteen months since she'd moved to Rumor from God-knew-where.

"What did you want to know, Deputy? I'd like to get back to what I was doing before you interrupted me."

He picked up his lemonade once again, casually swirling the liquid in the glass. He wasn't surprised that it was homemade. She looked the sort to make homemade lemonade on hot August afternoons. Truth be told, she looked the sort to be rocking babies and baking cookies. But it was her secretive nature that nagged at him. "Which was what?"

"None of your business."

He smiled faintly. "Is it me you don't like, or men in general?"

"What did you say your reason was for intruding on my afternoon?"

"Don't you *want* Harriet's murderer to be found, Molly?"

Her face paled a little. She carefully set aside her lemonade. "Of course I do."

"Then help me."

"Help you *what?*" She rose to her feet, hugging her arms around her as if it were cold outside, instead of just shy of Hades. "I've already told you everything I know. I went to Harriet's home that Monday because she hadn't shown up for work. It was completely unlike her, and though I'd called a few times, she didn't answer. So I drove over to her house because I was concerned. The door was unlocked and she was...was—"

Seated in a chair, a single .22 caliber GSW to the

head. The weapon that fired the shot was on the floor right beside her, intending to look like suicide. Chelsea Kearns, the forensics examiner who'd been called in on the case, had conclusively ruled this out.

"I don't need you to go over what you found again at Harriet's home, Molly," he said quietly.

The relief that crossed her face was nearly painful to see and more in keeping with her quiet blond prettiness than her barely veiled antagonism. "Then, I...I don't understand what you do want," she said. "I've already told you everything I know."

"Tell me what you don't know."

She looked at him, her eyes shadowed. "Shall I make up things, then? Is *that* the kind of law enforcement officer you are?"

"No, I don't want you to make up anything. Look." He sat forward, resting his wrists on his knees. "Sit down. Relax. Please," he finally added.

She slowly sat. Tugged her dress down closer to her knees again, as if she knew he had a hard time not looking at them. He could have told her that her smooth, lightly tanned calves and trim ankles, clad in tiny white socks were just as much a distraction, but figured it wouldn't help the situation. She already looked at him as if he were something to be scraped off her shoe.

"There's got to be something we're missing," he told her. "Harriet obviously had a private life that nobody knew about. She was four months pregnant at the time of her death. She didn't get that way by Immaculate Conception. And from everything that her sister, Louise Holmes, has told us, it doesn't seem as if Harriet was likely to have been artificially inseminated."

Molly's cheeks went pink, and for a minute he was in danger of losing his train of thought.

"You think the father of her baby killed her?"

Tessa Madison, the clairvoyant who'd been brought in by Harriet's nephew, Colby, had gotten the sense that Harriet was resisting an abortion. But Holt was more interested in physical evidence than psychic impressions. He didn't discount them, but a jury wasn't gonna convict on "feelings."

He rubbed his forehead, wondering at that moment why the hell he'd ever believed moving to Montana would be a lifesaver. "I think that there was more going on in Harriet's life than some people knew. Look at the way she had an ex-husband turn up."

"I read in the papers that Warren Parrish isn't a suspect, after all. He had an alibi or something, didn't he?"

Holt had liked Parrish a lot for the crime. But facts were facts and there was no way Parrish could have killed his former wife. "The more I find out about Harriet," he said, "the more complete a picture I can create of her life. The better I understand Harriet, the better I'll understand her murder."

"I can't think there is anything that would make murder understandable."

"Understandable. Not condonable."

"Do you have any other, um, suspects?"

Not one we can find. "I can't comment on that," he said.

For the first time, her lips twitched. "How wise of you, considering I'd hotfoot it right to the newspaper office to give them a scoop for the Monday-morning edition. Or worse, I might run immediately over to the Calico and blab your report."

"The news at eleven has nothing on the speed of the Rumor grapevine."

Her eyes met his in shared humor for the briefest of moments.

Even then it was too long.

He pulled his small notepad out of his pocket and deliberately thumbed through the pages. The humidity and heat was even having an effect on the thin pages. In some places his ink was smudging.

Harriet's writing had been smudged during the last moments of her life as she sat at her desk, he reminded himself grimly. She'd used only what she'd had available to her to leave behind three scrawled initials—a novel and her own blood. "Did Harriet keep a journal? A diary?"

"I told you before that I never saw one."

"Then you can tell me again."

Her shoulders visibly stiffened. "Why does this feel like an interrogation?"

Holt looked at her. "Trust me, Molly. If I were really interrogating you, you'd know it."

Her lashes swept down, and color suddenly rode high on her velvety cheeks. "It's you," she said suddenly. "I don't like *you.*"

He'd been a cop for more than fifteen years, and he had a fair ability to read people. Maybe that's why he could see that she was more surprised at the soft, fierce words that had escaped her lips than he was at hearing them. And for a moment he let himself focus on Molly Brewster. Not as an irritatingly inconvenient component of his investigation but as the puzzle that she was, all on her own.

Oh, yeah, she was surprised at the words that had popped out from her mouth. She was also bracing herself, as if she expected him to slam her in the hoosegow for speaking her mind.

"It's good to say what you feel." He picked up the lemonade and finished it off, wondering why his suspicious nature had taken that moment to step back in favor of wanting to put her at ease. It was just more evidence that when it came to women, his instincts were all messed up.

Her smooth forehead crinkled slightly. "Is it? I suppose you make a habit of doing so."

Now that was a laugh. "A diary, Molly. Or journal. Think about it. Did Harriet doodle on her desk pad at work?" Tessa had gotten some strong impressions when she'd been near Harriet's desk at the library. "Did she keep phone messages tucked away in a file? Confide in you over coffee on Monday morning before the library opened? Anything?"

"Harriet drank grapefruit juice in the mornings at the library, not coffee. And you already went over her office for evidence. Between you and the sheriff when he did it, you two practically tore the office apart. I even had to have some screws tightened on her desk because you'd worked the side piece loose."

He stifled an oath. She was secretive and she didn't like giving simple, straight answers. Well, hell, no wonder he wanted to take her to bed. She was like every other woman he'd had the misfortune to want. As far as he was concerned, it was like some cosmic joke on him. The only women he was attracted to were the very women he couldn't afford to trust. The kind that ended up putting him through a wringer before they were through.

The case, he coldly reminded himself. Concentrate on the case.

"Other than the morning when you went out to check on her, had you ever been at Harriet's house before?"

Her lips firmed. He waited, wondering if she'd have the nerve to lie, even though her face plainly showed it when she did. "Yes," she finally said.

"How many times?"

Her shoulders shifted. "I don't know."

"When?"

"Just after I moved here."

"Why?"

"To go over some details."

"Personal details?"

"No!" She wouldn't look at him. "About the job at the library."

"How *did* you get the job?"

"Harriet offered it to me."

"After you'd been banished to Rumor?"

"I wasn't *banished!* Rumor is a haven, not a prison." She'd jumped to her feet again.

A haven from what? "So you applied for the job after you moved here?"

"No."

"Then how did you get it? Apply by mail, phone, fax, e-mail?"

"I met Harriet at a conference and she offered me the job."

"Just like that."

Her teeth were clenched. "Just like that."

"So, at this conference, did you two hang out together? Hit happy hour with the rest of the ladies?"

"I didn't *hang out* with Harriet. And I seriously doubt she ever once went out to a happy hour."

He sat back, hitching his ankle up to his knee and lazily tapped the notepad on his bent leg. "Why?"

"She wasn't like that."

Frankly, based on his brief encounters with Harriet Martel before her death, he had a hard time seeing her as a barfly. She'd been brusque, albeit helpful enough, when he'd gone into the library for some reference material. Not until she'd died and he'd begun investigating her murder had stories of her quiet, kindhearted actions come to light to help counteract the image of the solitary woman. In her midforties, Harriet had been strong-willed, opinionated and not immediately personable, though she'd done a lot of kind things for other people.

"How do you know she wasn't like that?"

"I worked with her!"

"Yes, you did," he agreed softly. "Yet you expect me to believe that you and the victim didn't *once* have any kind of conversation that verged on personal matters. That she never confided in you, that you never overhead her confide in someone else. Come on, Molly, the library isn't *that* large. Your office even connected with hers."

She looked away, her jaw set. But it was too late; he'd already seen the sheen in her eyes that turned them from barely-there blue to glistening aquamarine. He pushed to his feet and moved around until he could see her face.

Between him, the two chairs and little table and the rail around the porch, she had no place to go, and he instinctively kept from crowding her any more than necessary. "What are you afraid of,

Molly? Do you suspect someone yourself? Just tell me. I'll protect you.''

Her head suddenly went back, and the part of him inside that hadn't turned to stone long ago went cold at the expression in her eyes.

''The last thing I need is a *cop* vowing protection.'' Scorn practically dripped from her tense body.

''Are you saying that you do know something? Molly, you can voluntarily help me or not. Either way, I'll get at the truth. Whatever you're hiding will come out.''

''Don't threaten me.''

''That's no threat.'' He lifted his hand, narrowing his eyes a little when she jerked back. He continued the movement, swiping away the spider that was busily spinning a line of web straight toward her shoulder. ''I always find my man. Or my woman.''

Her lips parted. ''Is that some sort of, of, *suggestion* that I had something to do with Harriet's death?'' Her voice rose a little.

''You did get a promotion.'' He waited a long beat, letting it sink in. ''People have killed for less.''

''You're vile.''

''I'm a deputy sheriff, ma'am,'' he said flatly. ''And there could well be a murderer right here in Rumor among us. If your sensibilities are offended, that's just too damn bad. Murder *is* a vile business.'' And if it took manipulating the jumpy, sexy woman into finding the murderer, then that was also too damn bad. There wasn't much that Holt believed in anymore. But he did believe in justice.

She moved suddenly, brushing past him despite the lack of space. It left him feeling even more scorched than from the afternoon heat. ''You are just as hateful as every other cop it's been my misfortune to know.'' She shoved open her door and disappeared inside.

The door slammed shut so hard the glasses on the little table rattled right along with the windows in their panes.

He picked up his glass and sucked down the lone, remaining ice cube as he studied the other glass. The one she'd used. It was still more than half-full.

There was a small, faint pink glisten smudged on the rim of the glass. She'd put gloss on her lips before she'd come out with the lemonade.

How many other cops have you known, Molly Brewster? And why?

He didn't believe for one minute that she was guilty of murdering her boss, or even conspiring to have her killed. He did know, right down to his bones, though, that she was hiding something.

And he needed to know what it was in case it had some bearing on the investigation.

Right now, the only strong suspects they had were Lenny Hostetler, whose whereabouts where unknown, and the father of Harriet's baby, whose complete identity was unknown.

Lenny had cause to be angry with Harriet because she'd helped his wife and children escape his abuse, and Darla Hostetler, said now-ex-wife, had strongly confirmed her belief that Lenny was more than capable of murder.

And the father of Harriet's baby? Who knew what kind of motive he might have had, if any. Maybe Tessa had been right, and the guy wanted Harriet to end the pregnancy. Maybe he'd been so desperate for that to happen that he'd been willing to kill the mother in the process.

Holt sighed and set down his glass. Without second guessing his reasons, barely touching the rim of Molly's glass, he scooted it to the edge of the table. Then, with one finger at the bottom edge, and the other on the top rim, he smoothly tipped the lemonade into his empty glass.

In the SUV that served as his patrol vehicle, he grabbed a fresh paper bag from the evidence kit in the back, and bagged the glass right along with the fingerprints on it that Molly Brewster had unwittingly left him.

Chapter Two

It was dark by the time Molly remembered the glasses she'd left on the front porch. She'd been so furious with Holt Tanner and his insane suggestion that she'd had something to do with Harriet's death that she'd spent the entire afternoon and early evening pummeling the earth in her tiny backyard.

She had the great makings for a garden by the time exhaustion finally forced her to stop. Of course, if Molly's sister had been around, she'd have wryly pointed out that planting a garden in Montana during the last harsh gasp of summer was probably a fruitless venture.

Rinsing off her gardening tools, Molly stored them in the little storage shed and headed around the side of the house, intending to get the glasses. There were some times that she missed her sister so badly, she ached with it.

If she could only call Christina. Hear her sister's voice. Molly would feel better about the path she'd chosen.

But she didn't dare call Christina. Nor could she e-mail her sister, or send a letter, or do anything at all that might possibly provide a trail back to Molly's location. It was safer for her, and certainly safer for Christina and her family, for things to remain just the way they'd been for the past eighteen months.

Which meant that Molly had nobody with whom she could share her worries. Nobody with whom she could vent her frustrations that she could even find a man in law enforcement remotely attractive. Not after all she'd been through with Rob.

Rounding the corner of the house, Molly went up the porch steps and grabbed the glass from the table. She didn't want to track mud from her shoes through the living room, so she started back down the porch steps to return to the back of the house and the entrance there that led into a tiny mudroom.

Just as she reached for the wooden screen door, though, she stopped cold. *One* glass.

She held it up to the light, gingerly peering at the glass as if it had turned into a snake.

The glass wasn't a snake, though. A certain deputy sheriff *was*.

No doubt in her mind at all that Holt Tanner had taken the other glass, she snatched open the screen door and grabbed her purse and car keys from where they were sitting on top of the washing machine.

Less than five minutes later, she'd driven up Main Street and pulled into the small parking area near the sheriff department. It was after eight o'clock in the evening and there was no earthly reason why she'd know that Holt Tanner would be at the station. But there he was. Just walking out the door, the light from inside shining over his dark hair, making it gleam like onyx.

You are in control. She climbed out of her car, and his head snapped up as if he'd sensed her. Though it was too dark and he was too far away to be sure, she was certain he was looking at her with that narrow-eyed, intense stare of his. Then he started toward her, moving with that curiously loose-limbed grace that seemed odd for someone who was always grim.

He stopped several feet away, his face in shadow. "Ms. Brewster. Something I can do for you this evening?"

Her hands curled. "You can give me back my glass that you stole this afternoon."

"Harsh words."

"True words. You had no right to take it. I can only imagine what you thought you would do with it. There are privacy laws in this country, you know."

He turned on his heel and started for an SUV parked several yards away.

She blinked and hurriedly shut her car door. "Hey. Don't ignore me!"

He kept right on walking until he reached the vehicle. Then he opened the door and leaned inside.

Irritation bubbled in her veins and she went right after him. "Deputy, do *not* ignore me. I won't have it, I tell you. Unless you're serious about me being a suspect in Harriet's death, you have absolutely no *right* to invade my privacy like you have. You have no possible way of knowing the trouble—" *He was inviting.* She barely contained the words and stood there, shuddering at her temerity.

He straightened and turned. "Believe me, Ms. Brewster, I wish I could ignore you." His lips were twisted as if he found something amusing about the situation. "Here."

He thrust out his hand, and she recoiled, realizing belatedly that he was handing her the paper sack he had in his hand. "What is it?"

"So suspicious," he murmured. "It's your glass."

Feeling like a fool, she snatched the sack from him. The thin paper crinkled under her tight grasp. "That's the pot calling the kettle black. You give *suspicious* new meaning."

"I'm doing my job, Ms. Brewster."

"Stop calling me that!" Her face flamed. She knew she was acting like an idiot, but there seemed nothing she could do about it. Outrageous words kept coming out of her mouth no matter how badly she wanted to contain them.

"All right. What would you prefer I call you?" He leaned back against the side of his truck and crossed his arms. Leisurely. As if they had all the time in the world.

Now the words stopped up in her throat.

He tilted his head slightly, watching her as if she were some kind of bug stuck on the end of a pin. "Maybe you'd prefer I use your real name," he suggested softly.

Molly's fingers tightened spasmodically, and the sack fell from her grasp. She stared as, almost in slow motion, it headed for the pavement. She couldn't even bring herself to move as glass, definitely *not* in slow motion, exploded from the bag like a perfectly rounded firework.

She heard a stifled oath, then nearly screamed when hands closed tightly over her hips. "Leave me alone!"

"Be still. You've got glass all over your legs."

He dumped her unceremoniously on the bench seat inside his truck and dropped his hand on her knee. When he leaned toward her, she sucked in a harsh breath and instinctively flattened herself back against the seat as far as she could go.

Holt went completely still. Panic rolled off her in waves strong enough to knock him flat, and a ball of fury formed inside him so rapidly that he felt sick to his stomach. Maybe Molly Brewster was secretive. Maybe she caused him no amount of personal consternation.

But he wanted to put his hands on whoever had hurt her and slowly choke the life out of him.

"I'm reaching for my flashlight," he said after a moment, when he could be sure his voice would come out without betraying the red haze burning in his head. "So I can see if the glass cut you." Moving slowly, he took his hand off her knee and stepped back a few inches. "It's right under the seat."

Her eyes were filled with shadows and bored into his face.

"Put your right hand down, Molly," he said softly. "You can't miss it. You'll feel it."

Her hands, clutched together at her waist, separated. She started to reach. Paused.

"It's one of those long-handled kind. Metal. Makes a good weapon in a pinch."

Her long lashes flickered. The pearly edge of her

teeth caught her upper lip. And slowly, so slowly that he hurt inside from it, she slid her right hand down the seat. A moment later she'd pulled out the foot-long flashlight. She dragged her gaze from his face to study the thing.

God only knew what was running through her mind. He supposed if she felt the need to slam it into him, he might even let her. The way he felt at the realization that someone had hurt her, *someone* needed to get maimed. "Heavy sucker, isn't it?"

She hefted it a little higher, pulling it up to her lap, knocking into the steering wheel as she did so. She jerked, and the flashlight rolled from her fingers.

He caught it and flicked it on, casually stepping back even more as he trained the light on her calves and ankles.

Dammit. She had several little pinpricks of blood right above the edge of her folded sock, which no longer looked white as snow as it had that afternoon. "You been out digging ditches?"

"What?" Her voice was barely audible.

"Your shoes and socks are muddy."

She lifted her hand, touching her forehead with fingers that trembled. "I was, um, d-digging out a garden."

"There's a first-aid kit under the seat, too. Did you finish the garden?" He kept his voice low. Easy. She was beginning to relax and he didn't want to jeopardize that.

"There's hardly any yard." She handed him the small white plastic box. "Left, I mean. I dug up so much."

"You must wield a mean shovel. My grandfather

would've loved you. Hold this so I can see what I'm doing."

"You had a grandfather."

His lips twisted a little as he hunkered down on his heels with the long tweezers from the kit and began fishing for tiny shards of glass. "Most people do," he said. "Though I've been accused a time or two of springing from some sort of pod." He gingerly plucked a tiny sliver from the taut skin of her slender shin. It was hard not to appreciate the shape of her limbs. They were about as perfect as legs could be.

"He had a place near Billings," he forced himself to continue. Anything to get her to relax. And knowing that he was doing as much admiring as he was removing slivers of glass wasn't going to get it. "I spent summers with him." His grandfather had been an ornery old coot, a farmer of sorts who loved his bottle almost as much as he'd loved his land.

In comparison to Holt's life in Los Angeles with his mother, who'd either been high on life and whatever man she'd brought home this time or high on something considerably more illegal, summers in Montana with that ornery old man had been as near to heaven as he'd figured he'd ever get.

"He's the reason I ended up in Montana," he told Molly. He sat back a bit. "Do you feel any glass in your legs still?"

She rotated her ankles. "I don't think so. I didn't to begin with. You, um, you came here from California, you said."

"Banished was the term you used, I think."

The flashlight's beam wavered under her hold

when she shifted. He looked up at her as he tore open another antiseptic pad.

"I shouldn't have said that."

"It's what you thought."

"It was cruel." Her voice went even softer. "I'm not usually cruel."

He dabbed at the cluster of tiny cuts on her leg. They oozed tiny droplets of blood and he tore open several plastic bandages. "Yeah, well, I bring that out in a lot of people."

"There's no excuse."

"Honey, there is *always* an excuse." His lips twisted. "And I've probably heard 'em all over the years."

The toe of her shoe lifted slowly while he stuck the bandages in place. "Deputy?"

He looked up as he smoothed down the last bandage. "Yeah?"

"How did you know?"

He glanced down at her feet. They were still again. He wasn't entirely sure he trusted them to stay that way and he had no particular desire to take a size-six tennis shoe in the face. But take it he would, before he'd lift a hand against her. "About your name?"

She nodded stiffly.

"I wasn't certain." He judiciously gave her feet clearance as he began gathering up the stuff from the first-aid kit. "Until now."

Her lips parted. "You bas—"

"Yeah." He straightened. "Literally and metaphorically." Letting her chew on that, he stuck the closed kit in her hands. "Put that back, would you?"

Those impossibly black lashes of hers lowered for

a moment as her fingers tightened on the hard, plastic box. He could practically see the urge to heave it at him playing out in her mind.

After a long moment she sighed and slipped the box back under the seat. "I haven't done anything wrong. I'm not a criminal or anything. And I didn't hurt Harriet. I've never hurt anyone."

"But you're running. From someone."

"I'm not running." Her throat worked and her voice went hoarse. "I'm living."

He raked his hands through his hair. What was it about this woman that got so thoroughly under his skin? So *rapidly* under his skin?

It was a bad sign.

"Molly, whoever it is could be a suspect. You've got to realize that."

"That's impossible. Nobody knows that I'm here."

"Family?"

Her eyes suddenly glistened. He harshly reminded himself that women conjured tears at the drop of a hat. She was probably running from whoever had hurt her—a husband, a lover, a father. God only knew. Maybe she was even one of Lenny Hostetler's conquests. They seemed to be cropping up with amazing regularity considering the guy had seemingly disappeared from the planet. Molly certainly looked Lenny's type. The little worm of a man unfailingly went for slender blondes.

But that didn't mean Molly was any more trustworthy than any other woman who'd ever been in his life.

Molly Brewster isn't in your life.

"My family knows nothing."

He leaned against the opened door. "Must be pretty bad if you've cut your family out of your life, too. Seems that person might have cause to be mad at Harriet for helping you find a new life."

She stared at him, her expression stony. "Did you take my fingerprints off that glass? Is that why you stole it?"

Obviously, she was recovering from her shock well enough. "Borrowed. I planned to return it."

"After you'd taken my fingerprints from it, I presume."

"Yes."

She looked as if she was struggling with temper. Or tears. Maybe both. "Did you?"

"Get your print? Yes."

Tears won out. Glistening tears clung to her dark lashes, looking like liquid jewels. "I told you I've done nothing wrong!"

"But you're scared to death I'm going to run the print. What'll I find when I do?"

Her gaze sought his. She leaned forward, her hands digging into the seat beside her legs. "You haven't done that yet?"

"No. Not yet."

"If you try, I'll...I'll sue you!"

"Will you?"

Her gaze flickered, and he nearly smiled. Except there was little satisfaction in manipulating this particular situation. His only justification was that there was a murderer out there, and Holt wanted him caught. If it took a little manipulation of this woman, then so be it. "Not if you help me."

"That's blackmail. Or extortion or something! I should have known not to expect better."

"That's cooperation," he countered smoothly. "I help you, you help me. In the end we both win, don't we?"

"I don't like you."

"You don't have to. All you have to do is help me."

"What if I go to the sheriff and complain about this?"

"Knock yourself out." He pulled out his cell phone. "Want me to dial for you?"

She practically recoiled from the phone. "I don't want to talk to the sheriff!"

He pocketed the phone. "Somehow, that doesn't surprise me."

"You're hateful."

"And you're my only real link to Harriet Martel."

"You're overestimating my knowledge of her."

"It's a possibility," he conceded. "Though a damned slim one in my opinion. You worked at least forty hours a week for more than a year and a half with her. As far as I'm concerned that means you were as close to her as anyone else I've been able to find. Now, do we have a deal or not?"

"I don't seem to have much of a choice."

"Is that a yes?"

She looked away and seemed to be watching the darkened town park across the way. Either that, or the library, which was also across the street.

"I don't like your tactics, Deputy. Why should I trust you to hold up your end of this? For all I know, you're already running my fingerprint against every databank into which the sheriff department is linked."

"I don't lie." Not exactly.

"Nor do I."

"You're lying about your identity."

"That's survival," she said flatly.

He'd figured as much, given the sum of her reactions since they'd met. "I'll return your print when I finish my investigation. That's the best I can do."

"Maybe I'll just leave town." Her voice shook, the bravado thin.

"If you do, then I'll list you as an official suspect, hunt you down and drag your sweet butt right back here to Rumor. And your days of privacy and assumed identity are over."

"You wouldn't. You're supposed to be looking for Harriet's *killer,* not wasting time with innocent citizens like me!"

"Exactly. I don't care whether you like my tactics or not, Molly. I want her killer found."

She was shaking, and her face was pale as moonlight. But her eyes, even in the shadowy night, nearly shot sparks at him as she slid off the high seat. "Fine," she whispered stiffly. Then she turned on her heel and walked back to her little car.

Holt watched her fumble with the door handle, then climb behind the wheel and, after a couple tries before the engine caught, drive out of the small parking lot.

He'd won.

Except there was no feeling of victory inside him at all.

Chapter Three

Molly unlocked the main doors of the library and went inside, flicking on the overhead lights as she went. She refused to look over her shoulder at the building across the street that housed the city offices, including the sheriff department and the mayor's office.

You are in control.

She snorted softly as she pushed aside a book cart that one of the volunteers had left sitting in the aisle between the circulation desk and the administrative offices behind it. "Control? What a joke."

She slapped the light switch on the wall just inside the main office and stared at Harriet's office. There was a large, ancient desk that took up most of the space. Edwardian, Harriet had once told Molly. But pretty much ruined for its antique value when some owner along the way had added the "custom" sidepiece to use as a typewriter return. Harriet had purchased it secondhand for a song. It was big and it was ugly. And without Harriet behind it, it looked sad. It was also still piled with work that Harriet had never had a chance to attend to.

Several boxes of old-looking, dusty books were stacked on the floor against the wall. And a small stack of hardcover books sat on the sidepiece of her desk right next to the typewriter that looked to be as old as Molly was. The library did possess a computer system. There was a terminal at the circulation desk, one in the reference section and one in Molly's office that also tied into an international interlibrary system. But Harriet had flatly refused to have one in her office despite the convenience it offered.

"I loathe the things. Making people smarter on one hand and dumber than dirt on the other."

Molly smiled sadly, easily imagining Harriet's brusque tones. "You saved my life once already, Harriet," she whispered to the empty office. "Tell me what to do now."

Only silence greeted her.

Sighing again, Molly went to the smaller office next door and tucked away her purse in the bottom drawer of her desk. She flipped open her calendar, glancing over the activities scheduled for the day. Her attention was barely on it, though. Not when she half expected Holt Tanner to come striding through the library doors at any moment.

When he hadn't done so by closing time that evening, Molly's tension had reached new heights.

"Could we have a little quiet here?" Her voice was sharper than she intended, and the group of teenagers sitting around one of the study tables looked up at her in shock. D.J. Reingard stopped tapping his oversize pencil against the table and frowned a little. "Sorry, Ms. Brewster. We're just finishing the plans for the fund-raisers."

Molly knew that. She pressed her fingertips to the cool wooden table, silently cursing her bad mood on Holt Tanner. "I'm sorry, D.J. You guys are fine. I guess the heat is getting to me."

D.J. looked at her even more oddly, as it was cool as a spring evening inside the new library facility. She certainly wasn't going to tell him that the newest deputy his father, the sheriff of Rumor, had hired was driving her right around the bend. "So, what did you all decide on? A rummage sale or a bake sale?"

The group of teens was conducting a summer project to help raise funds to reestablish a bookmobile program that would help serve the children and families in some of the more remote ranching areas around Rumor. Molly was all for the program and, with Harriet's blessing, had been working with this particular group of honor students for the better part of the year. So far they'd raised thousands of dollars through a Halloween carnival, holiday crafts and baked goods, Christmas wreaths and a half dozen other, smaller projects.

"Both," Becky Reed answered with a grin. She was a petite redhead with a spray of freckles across her nose and a crush for D.J. the size of Montana. D.J., however, seemed to only have eyes for one of the other girls in the group—a statuesque sixteen-going-on-thirty blonde named Tiffany.

"We want to do it in two weeks," D.J. said, pulling his brilliant blue gaze from Tiffany to focus on

Molly. "We can still use the parking lot here at the library, right?"

Molly nodded. "Are you sure you'll be able to gather up enough donations in that short amount of time, though? School will be starting right after that, too."

The kids—ten in all—around the table nodded. D.J. grinned, and Molly could easily see why Becky was smitten. He was seventeen, smart, athletic, blond and about as good-looking as a male could be.

Rob had been blond and blue-eyed, too. As handsome as a movie star, and as cold as the dark side of the moon.

She pushed aside the unwelcome thought. Ever since Harriet's death, Molly's memories of Rob had been stirred up. Nightmares in which Rob was the killer and Molly the victim, sleepless nights, near panic attacks. She was almost as much a wreck as she had been when she'd first escaped to Rumor.

She realized the kids were all chattering, and forced herself to focus.

"My mom has been nagging us to clean out the attic and the garage," D.J. was saying. "There's enough junk there to supply five rummage sales." He rolled his eyes and grinned. "It's a win-win situation. Mom gets off our case about the stuff, and we get a few more bucks for the bookmobile project."

"I'll bet we can get Libby Adler to donate some brownies or cookies or something, too."

"Jessup," Becky corrected the other girl who'd spoken. "She and Marcus Jessup got married during the Crazy Moon Festival, remember? In a double-wedding ceremony with Nick Sullivan and Callie Griffin.''

"Nick Sullivan is a hunk." Tiffany spoke up for the first time. "But that Mr. Jessup is totally creepy if you ask me. I bet Libby Adler married him just 'cause of his oodles of money. It definitely wasn't for his looks. Those scars on his face? Totally scary.''

Becky's eyes narrowed. "I cannot believe even *you* are so stupid, Tiffany. I swear, you may be on the honor roll, but you don't have the sense God gave a stump.''

Tiffany looked bored, but Becky wasn't done. And frankly, Molly could hardly blame her. Tiffany was a constant trial with her snooty ways.

"Mr. Jessup's first family died in a fire," Becky was saying scathingly. "That's how he got those *minor* scars. When he was trying to save them.''

Tiffany smirked. "Shows what you know, Becky Reed. I heard he was suspected of killing his first wife.''

Molly had heard enough. "Tiffany—"

"That's enough," D.J. cut in. "Mr. Jessup has donated a lot to this town. My dad says he provided the new computer system at the sheriff's department and didn't even want anyone to know about it. And it's true what Bec said about him trying to save 'em.''

Tiffany's bright-blue eyes suddenly flooded with tears and she looked imploringly at D.J. "I'm sorry," she whispered, and wrapped her long fingers around his arm. "You're right, of course, D.J.''

Most of the kids around the table looked uncomfortable. Molly caught Becky rolling her eyes the moment before she shoved back from the table. "Are we done here?" the girl asked tartly.

Whether the rest of the group figured they were or not, Molly stepped in and made sure of it as she reminded them of their next meeting and told them where they could begin storing items collected for the sale.

Then, with a cacophony of chair legs scraping against the hard floor, the group left en masse, a hoard of basically good kids dressed in everything from blue jeans to bikini tops and shorts dragging purses, backpacks, skateboards and computerized games along with them.

"I'd heard you were working with a group of kids from the high school."

Molly whirled at the deep voice that came from behind her. "Don't sneak up behind me." Her voice was sharp. Shaking.

"Came right through the main doors, Molly."

Holt walked over to the long, rectangular table and picked up one of the chairs that had been left haphazardly scattered and placed it back at the table. She watched him, torn between suspicion and irritation and something else she didn't even want to put a name to. She knew what it was to fear a man. She didn't fear Holt, though.

Not…exactly.

Molly began straightening the rest of the chairs surrounding the table and collecting up the various magazines and books that had been left on top of it. Familiar tasks. Soothing tasks.

Tasks that didn't occupy her thoughts anywhere near enough to distract her from the deputy.

She kept stealing looks at him from the corner of

her eye. He wasn't wearing his typical uniform today. In fact, he wore a suit. Nothing flashy for the solemn deputy. Medium-gray suit. Blinding-white shirt. The tie was a surprise, though.

"Surfboards?" The observation popped out of her mouth. He hadn't dragged it loose at the collar the way he had his tie yesterday when he'd invaded her Sunday afternoon.

He glanced down, flipping the tie slightly between his long fingers. The pattern in the swirling gray-and-black silk was actually stylized waves complete with surfer and surfboards, something she'd only been able to pick out as she'd rounded the end of the table near where he stood.

"My partner's wife back in L.A. had a weird sense of humor," he said with a crooked smile, and Molly felt her nerves tighten oddly.

She turned and shoved her armful of books and magazines onto the book cart. She didn't want to notice that his smile, faint though it was, made the intimidating man seem momentarily approachable. Human.

He gave no explanation for the reason for his suit, she noticed. Not that she expected one. Not that she wanted one. He was forcing her into helping him with his case, whether she could really be helpful or not.

She didn't care what the man had been doing all day. She really and truly did not. "I'm surprised you weren't here snooping the moment the doors opened this morning." She wanted to kick herself. She began pushing the cart toward periodicals, simply to get away from the deputy and the appalling lack of sense she seemed to have around him.

"I had to be in Whitehorn for a case."

Harriet's? She wanted to ask, but by firmly tucking her tongue between her teeth managed to refrain. She began shelving the magazines, annoyed that he'd followed her right between the high shelves. It was dark and dim and he seemed to suck all the air right out of the area.

Okay, it wasn't dark. It wasn't dim, she silently acknowledged as she crouched down to reach the bottom shelf. But he still made the area seem that way. Too close. Way too close.

She shot to her feet and pushed the cart rapidly down the row. The front wheel—the one that shimmied a little—squealed loudly. "You know where Harriet's office is, Deputy," she said, speaking over the noise. "There's no point following me back here. Harriet didn't shelve materials herself. I doubt she hid any secrets of her life back here."

She clipped the corner of the next shelf with the wheel of her book cart.

"Think maybe you need a license to drive this thing."

He was standing right behind her, his hands nudging hers away from the push bar of the cart.

She jumped away, then flushed like the ninny she obviously was. "I—" *don't know what to say.*

His dark eyes watched her. Waited.

She pressed her lips together and slid between the book cart and the shelving, moving ahead of it, and grabbed up a handful of magazines. It was fortunate that she could nearly do this particular task in her sleep.

He followed along, the book cart moving slowly behind her. Of course the wheel behaved for *him*.

They went up one row. Down another. From periodicals to nonfiction. From there to fiction.

If she thought waiting for his arrival had been nerve-racking, it was nearly torturous having him close on her heels, his thoughts kept close to himself, well hidden by those unreadable brown eyes.

She wondered for a moment if she'd lose her job if word got out at the way she ran, screaming madly, from the library one hot summer day. Shaking off the absurdity, she turned to the cart only to stop short in surprise.

"You're finished."

She looked from the empty book cart that separated them to his face. "Well, this particular task is completed, at least."

"Molly."

She jerked, whirling around to see one of the volunteers standing behind her with a frankly curious gaze that took in both Molly and the deputy. She needed to get a grip. "Yes, Mrs. English?"

"It's five," the elderly woman said gently. "I wanted to let you know I was leaving."

Five? Molly managed a smile and thanked the woman as she left. Then she looked over her shoulder at Holt. Just as quickly she looked away. The man was too disturbing by far. "I've got to close up. I hadn't realized it was so late." She began rolling the book cart to its proper place.

"What's the rush? You're often here after five."

She shoved the cart into its spot beneath a counter. "How did you know that? Spying on me?"

"This place is across from the sheriff department." His voice was mild. "My desk is next to the window in the front. Simple observation makes you paranoid?''

Rob had kept track of every single thing she'd done, every single person with whom she'd had contact. She'd had no privacy, and he'd made darned sure that she knew it.

''I have plans this evening.'' She had to step around him to go to her office.

He followed. ''You haven't moved your stuff into Harriet's office.''

She leaned over to retrieve her purse from the bottom drawer in the desk. ''Is there some law against that?''

''What's with the defensiveness?''

Courtesy of her foot, the drawer shut a little harder than necessary. She straightened, hugging her purse to her. ''Nothing.'' Just because she'd been told more than once by the trustees that she needed to switch offices in order to make room for a new assistant librarian really was no reason to take it out on the deputy. Even if she did consider him quite responsible for making her a nervous wreck. ''I'd think you'd be glad, considering everything, that Harriet's office is still just the way she left it. Ought to ease your search for clues into her private life.''

''Her office isn't the connection I need. It's you. Thought we'd established that.''

''Well,'' she grabbed her keys and walked past him, snapping off lights as she made her way to the entrance, ''you're just going to have to wait now. Because I'll be busy all evening.''

He caught hold of the entrance door before she could open it. ''Doing what?''

She looked above her head at his hand, the large

square palm, the long, blunt-edged fingers, and swallowed down a jolt. It was just a hand. A man's hand. A cop's hand.

"I have, a, uh, a reading group I meet with on Monday evenings." It was more or less the truth and was certainly all she intended to divulge to this particular man.

"Are there a lot of reading groups?"

"A few." She tugged at the door and relaxed some when he moved his hand, allowing her to open it. "I think it was kind of a new concept here in Rumor, but they're getting more popular." She waited for him to move out of the way before locking it up.

"Did Harriet meet with any groups?" He easily kept up with her as she hurried to her car.

"Not really. And none of the groups include any men yet, so if that's where your thoughts are heading, don't bother." She tossed her purse across the seat and sat down, wincing a little at the hot, vinyl interior. She cranked down her window, trying not to look at the deputy.

He was standing beside the car, his expression as serious as it always was. She really didn't want to notice the way his finely woven trousers tightened across his hips because of the hand he'd shoved in one pocket, or the way his silly tie lay against a chest that looked hard even through the severely white shirt he wore. So, of course, that was exactly what she noticed. That, and the way his eyes didn't look quite so densely brown because the sunlight—still bright and hot even at that hour—was shining almost directly in his face.

His thick, spiky lashes were narrowed around that

gleam of coffee-brown that seemed focused directly on her.

"Are you always so intense?" Her face flamed and she cursed her wayward tongue.

He closed his hands over the door, seeming oblivious to the hot metal, and leaned down a little so he could look into the car. "When I'm after something I want."

His hair truly was black, she thought faintly. There wasn't the least bit of gold, nor red, nor brown in the thick shock of it that looked in danger of tumbling over his forehead if not for the way it was brushed severely back from his hard face.

She needed therapy. That's all there was to it. She absolutely, positively could *not* be physically attracted to this man. She could *not* be wondering if he brought that single-minded focus into matters of the personal kind.

The intimate kind.

She hadn't felt a flicker of desire for anyone in so long that she wasn't even sure that's what she was feeling now. Only the curling in her stomach as she dragged her gaze from the very masculine hands not ten inches from her shoulder made a mockery of that particular notion.

"And you want Harriet's killer," she finished. It took two tries before she managed to fit her key in the ignition.

He was silent so long that she turned to look at him. Only to find that intense gaze focused on her face once more.

Her mouth ran dry and she swallowed. Reminded herself harshly that this man, *Deputy* Holt Tanner,

represented everything that she'd left. No, that she'd
been forced to flee.

"Yeah. I want her killer." His lips twisted. "I
want…a lot of things. But that'll do for now." He
straightened and thumped the door with his palm before finally removing his hands. "Have fun with your
reading group. I'll be by the library first thing tomorrow."

Then he was stepping away from the car, sliding
off his jacket and hitching it over his shoulder with
his thumb as he walked away.

She closed her eyes for a moment, willing her
heart to stop racing, her stomach to stop jumping.
When she opened them again, the deputy was no
longer in sight.

She told herself she was glad.

Chapter Four

Holt saw Molly's car on the side of the highway and immediately slowed, pulling up behind her.

It was nearly midnight. He'd followed her when she'd left the library. He hadn't expected to make a second trip into Whitehorn that day, but that's where she headed, so that's where he'd followed. As far as he was concerned, the second trip was a lot more worthwhile than the wild-goose chase that Dave Reingard had sent him on for the first one.

Once Molly reached *her* destination that evening, for three hours he'd sat in his dust-covered truck far enough away to avoid suspicion outside a large house that he happened to know was a domestic-abuse shelter. He grimly speculated over what Molly was doing inside.

Reading group?

He'd doubted it.

Once he'd seen her leave—she'd stood in the front and chatted for a solid twenty minutes with two other women before driving away—he'd left his truck and walked over to the shelter where he'd had a brief chat with the director of the facility.

Angel Ramirez had been annoyingly close-mouthed. The only useful thing she had imparted was her comment that there were some volunteers—women who'd escaped their lives of abuse—who met with the current residents in group sessions to help reinforce their belief in a life other than what they'd been enduring.

Afterward he'd pulled into a coffee shop and stared into a cup of coffee, his twisted mind easily conjuring images of the kinds of horrors that those "volunteers" had probably endured.

That Molly had endured.

There was a time when Holt would have gone into a bar and tossed back a shot or two of whiskey to dull the images. But not anymore. He'd given up drinking around the same time he'd given up a lot of other things.

When he finally hit the road, he sure as hell hadn't expected to come across Molly's car on the highway, long after she'd already departed Whitehorn.

She should have been home, safe and sound in bed.

The relief he felt when his headlights illuminated the shape of her sitting behind the wheel was all out of proportion. Yeah, it was late. And yeah, she was a good fifteen miles outside of Rumor. He would be concerned about the safety of any woman stopped alone like this on the side of a highway.

The rationalizations were sound, the relief inside him way beyond rationalizing.

He left the engine and the lights going, and walked up the side of the road, giving her plenty of time to see him.

Her window was rolled down, and he could see her fingers flexing around the steering wheel. Her face was a wash of ivory, her hair a gleam of moonlight as she turned to look at him when he stopped beside the car.

"Having problems?"

At least she wasn't startled by him. Nor did she look exactly thrilled to see him.

"The engine quit."

"Have you called a tow?"

The glance she cast him was brief. "Yes, Deputy, I called a tow. I stuck my head out the window and yelled at the very top of my voice. I'm sure someone heard and will be along shortly."

"You don't have a cell phone."

"No."

"Nearly everyone has a cell phone these days."

"I don't. Nobody needs to call me."

"And there is nobody *you* need to call."

"Assistant librarians don't earn enough money to spend it on unnecessary luxuries."

"You're head librarian now. And what about emergencies like this?"

"I could have walked."

"In the middle of the night? Fifteen miles?"

"If I had to."

She might, at that, he thought, and refrained from giving her the lecture about safety that automatically sprang to mind. "Pop the hood."

"Why?"

He shoved his fingers through his hair. The woman could give lessons in being suspicious. Not that he was one to talk. "To see if we can't get this bucket of bolts going again."

"My car is *not* a bucket of bolts." Her voice was defensive. Nevertheless, he heard the distinctive pop of the hood release when she pulled it.

He bent over a little, looking past her into the car at the dash.

She stiffened like a shot. "What are you doing?"

"Making sure your gas gauge isn't reading empty."

"I'm not that foolish."

But she might have been that distracted. Along with Angel Ramirez's other miserly details, she had told him the group session that night had been particularly grueling.

He headed back to his truck. The opening of her car door was easily audible over the engine he'd left running.

"You're not l-leaving?"

"No." He pulled open his door and retrieved his flashlight. He flicked it on. "Remember this?"

The light from his headlights easily illuminated her face, along with the tangle of emotions that crossed it. Relief. Despair.

God. Of all the women for him to jones over, she had to be the most unsuitable.

He walked back to her car and lifted the hood.

She followed, and even though she kept a good distance between them, he was still damnably aware of her. The way she sucked in the corner of her lower lip as she'd look at him when she thought he was unaware. The way a few strands of hair had worked loose of the knot at the back of her head to cling to the delicate line of her jaw, the paleness of her neck.

He glared at the engine, wanting to ask her about the shelter, knowing she'd have a fit if she knew he'd followed her. As if her car had heard his thoughts, the narrow brace slipped and the hood crashed down on his shoulder.

He swore under his breath while Molly jumped back with a gasp. She hurriedly reached out, her hands knocking into his as they both reached for the brace to lift the hood off him.

He heard the way she sucked in her breath, and wanted to swear at the way she yanked her hand back. He was no prize, he'd be the first to admit it. But he wasn't used to women being *afraid* of him. Not unless they were walking on the wrong side of the law.

"Are you all right?"

"Yeah. But hold this," he muttered, and pushed the flashlight into her hands. "So I can see what I'm doing," he added pointedly.

She made a soft huff and redirected the beam from his eyes to the engine.

He stared hard, waiting until the spots in front of his eyes disappeared, then began checking hoses and belts. He found the problem quickly enough. "You need a new fan belt. For that matter, you ought to have the whole thing tuned up."

"Do-re-mi," she murmured.

He caught himself from smiling as he lowered the hood. "Lock it up. I'll drive you back to town."

"You can't fix it?"

He didn't know whether to be flattered that she'd

thought he might be able to or amused that she seemed peeved that he couldn't. "Yeah, I could. With the right parts." He took the flashlight from her and turned it off. "I'm not carrying even the wrong parts."

"Only flashlights and first-aid kits."

And evidence-collection kits, he thought. One that contained the print he'd lifted from her drinking glass. There was a part of him that wanted to run that print no matter what so-called agreement he'd struck with the woman.

There was a part of him that wanted to forget he'd ever taken the damned thing in the first place.

"Do you need help with anything?" He glanced at the lumps sitting on the passenger seat.

"No." Her voice was sharp. Defensive. If he'd been back in L.A., he'd have wondered just what was in that briefcase and enormous purse that would cause a driver to be so antsy with a cop. But he wasn't in Los Angeles anymore. And thank God for it.

He was standing on the side of a deserted highway in the middle of the night with a woman he wanted but couldn't trust, even if he *could* get past her thick defenses.

"Suit yourself." Leaving her to deal with her car, he went back to his truck and radioed in for a tow. Then he sat there, wrist propped over his steering wheel, as he watched her through the windshield.

The soft-sided briefcase she hefted over one shoulder looked heavy enough to knock her over, and he muttered an oath and shoved open the door and strode over to her.

"Don't argue. There are some things you're just

going to have to put up with when it comes to me,'' he said flatly as he slid the strap from her shoulder and took it. ''What's in here? Bricks?''

She pulled the second bag out of the car and slammed the door shut. ''Books. For the reading group, remember? I told you I could manage it.''

The reading group story again. Right. Angel Ramirez hadn't said squat about a reading group. ''So you did. Am I complaining about it?''

''I—'' She looked up at him, her expression guarded. ''I'm sorry. I thought you were.''

''I wasn't.'' He headed toward his truck. When she stayed right where she was, he looked back at her. Standing beside her twenty-year-old car, clutching her enormous carpetbag of a purse to her with both hands, the faint night breeze barely enough to stir the hem of her floaty pink dress about her shapely knees.

She'd spent her entire Monday evening with a group of women living at a shelter. She still had a small plastic strip on her shin that he figured he recognized.

He let out a long breath. ''Come on, Molly,'' he said quietly. ''Stop expecting the worst. Everything is going to be fine.''

Her fine eyebrows drew together. ''With my car, you mean.''

''Yeah. Right.''

She hesitated a moment longer, then walked to his truck. She stowed her purse on the floor by her feet and carefully nudged aside the jacket of his suit as if she might catch something from it.

She didn't speak until the lights of Rumor were

visible through the windshield. "Thank you for stopping."

"All part of being a public servant."

She made a noncommittal sound that grated on his nerves. He took the exit down to Main Street. "Your car will be towed sometime tonight."

"Oh, but—"

"I called it in already."

Her lips started to tighten up.

"I know you're perfectly capable of doing it yourself."

She absorbed that, and slowly lost the tight-lipped expression. "As long as I didn't spend the night sitting on the side of the highway, trying to decide the best course of action," she finally admitted. "What were you doing out there, anyway? Surely you weren't still on duty. Not after having been in Whitehorn all afternoon like you said. You haven't even changed out of your suit. Your jacket is probably unforgivably wrinkled from lying on the seat in a heap the way it is."

He was saved from coming up with an answer when he pulled up in front of her house. "Here you go. Will you need a ride to work in the morning? I could send around a car—"

"No!" She hurriedly gathered up her purse. "Of course I don't need a ride. It's just a few blocks around the park. A nice walk, in fact. I do wish the heat would let up, though. I keep telling myself that in a month, when the weather has really turned, I'll be wishing for a little heat."

She was speaking fast. Too fast. Making him wonder what had set her into this latest panic. He got out to carry in that enormous bag of books of hers. "Sure it's a nice walk as long as you don't have to cart this thing back to the library.''

Her expression lightened a little. If he wasn't mistaken, she *almost* smiled. Which, of course, there in the middle of the godforsaken ninety-degree night made him determined to see just what that might look like. A real smile on Molly Brewster's face when she looked at him.

Knowing he was probably one of the last people on earth to be able to succeed at that annoyed him no end.

She was fumbling a little with her keys. "Fortunately, the books are mine," she assured as she finally pushed open the front door. "They get to stay here. Um, thank you, again, Deputy. For the ride, and all.''

Once again she stood squarely in the doorway. Not budging an inch, telling him absolutely that she was not going to invite him in. Not for coffee. Not for discussion about Harriet. Not for…anything.

"We never did get around to talking much about Harriet.''

"Well, it's a little late tonight, and you warned me earlier today that you'd be by the library in the morning. Call me selfish, Deputy, but I'm thinking rather longingly of my bed.''

She wasn't the only one. The thought darkened his mood even more.

He deliberately reached past her to dump the heavy briefcase just inside the front door. "D'ya ever let anyone in your house, Molly? Let down that guard of yours enough to let someone in?''

She went still. "Is that pertinent to your investigation?''

He pushed his hands into his pockets where they couldn't do any damage to either of their peace of mind. "No."

"Then it's really none of your business."

He'd expected no other answer. Didn't have to mean he liked it, though. Or had to acknowledge the least bit of sting. "Be available to help me tomorrow. I want to go through Harriet's office again. Her desk, her files. Everything." He turned to go.

"Deputy, wait." She caught his arm, her touch too light to have the impact it did. "You've, um, you have a tear in your shirt. It must have happened when the hood of my car hit you." She slipped under his arm, and he felt her fingers probing his shoulder. "There's blood, too. Why didn't you say something?"

"I wasn't thinking about my shoulder."

"I think the tear is right there at the seam. It should be easy to fix. But you should soak it right away to get the stain out."

He was too old to get turned on by a woman just from a fleeting, simple touch. Had his partner still been alive to witness the way Holt nearly scrambled off the porch away from the blonde, he'd have laughed himself into a coma.

As it was, Molly was staring at him with dismay. "I'm sorry. Is it painful?"

He felt like choking. "Excuse me?"

"Your back. You jumped when I touched the spot where you were bleeding. I thought—"

"It's fine." He cleared his throat. "Fine. Don't worry about it."

Her lashes drifted down, then up again. "Well, it

was my car that did it. The least I can do is fix your shirt.''

''Don't sweat it, Molly. It's just a shirt. I've got a closetful of them.''

''Of silk shirts?'' Her eyebrows rose. ''They must be paying cops better than I remember. Come on, Deputy. I'd rather fix your shirt than have to buy you a new one. I'm on a budget, remember?''

Her lips weren't drawn up all tight and prudish now. She wasn't avoiding looking at him. She looked a little ornery and a lot determined.

''How would you know anything about what a cop earns?''

''I...don't. I just assumed.''

''You shouldn't lie, Molly,'' he told her flatly. ''Your face gives you away every single time.''

Now, he could add *stony* to the list of expressions on her face. ''I'm really quite weary already with your accusations, Deputy. Liar. Killer.''

''I know you didn't kill Harriet.'' He knew he sounded impatient, and he really didn't want to scare this woman, when it was so obvious that she shrank into herself whenever he raised his voice the least little bit. But some things a man couldn't help. His voice got a little louder when he was pissed, annoyed and aroused.

Only question was, which of the two of them he was more annoyed with—her or him.

Probably him. For having the disgustingly bad judgment to get the least bit involved with this woman.

A witness, for God's sake.

A woman ten years his junior.

A woman with lies that sat badly on her soft, pink

lips and painful secrets that lurked in her pale, pale-blue eyes.

He deliberately, carefully, kept his tone low. "I also know you're hiding a past that may be relevant." And if the woman would just open up to him a little bit about it, maybe he'd be able to help them both.

"We've played this song before, I believe. And we were talking about your shirt, anyway."

"Forget about it."

"I always pay my debts."

He dragged the shirt over his head, not even bothering with the buttons, except the top two, and tossed it to her.

She gaped at him. But she caught the shirt as it fluttered toward her.

"You wanna sew the shirt, fine," he said, his voice hard. "Sew your little heart out. While you're doing it, you might try thinking about the debt that you may owe Harriet. Maybe then something will come to you that will help me find the person who *did* kill her."

He turned and walked back to his truck, the vision of her slender fingers tangled in his shirt burning into his mind.

Chapter Five

"Sue, are you sure that report on the treads hasn't come back from the Feds yet?"

"Good morning to you, too." Sue Gerhardt was the dispatcher and, Holt knew, the glue that held the small department together. "And, no, it hasn't. I called the FBI folks yesterday afternoon to follow up on it, too."

Here was a woman who was completely aboveboard. Helpful. Intelligent. "Anyone ever tell you you're the perfect woman, Sue?"

"Sure, my husband. How do you think he's managed to keep me for forty years?"

Holt smiled and headed for the coffeepot, giving a brief wave to Dave through his boss's glass-windowed office as he went. Dave nodded, his attention obviously taken with the phone call he was on.

"Anything interesting come in overnight?"

"Other than a call from a shelter in Whitehorn that some deputy from down here had been there last night nosing around, asking questions? Not a thing." Sue's sixty-two-year-old eyes were sharp. "Don't suppose you want to share, do you?"

"Sue, I'd share my heart with you if I still had one." He headed over to his desk by the window that overlooked the library.

Sue laughed. "Yeah, you're a heartless California boy, all right. I'm on to you, Holt Tanner. Big bad cop, my big toe. Did your little foray into Whitehorn have anything to do with the rumor going around that Harriet had helped some woman escape an abusive husband?"

Not in the way Sue might think, Holt thought. He'd been there because of Molly. But Sue didn't know that. She was thinking about Lenny.

Lenny Hostetler *had* been plenty angry with Harriet Martel for helping his wife and kids escape their life with him. Maybe even angry enough to cause her harm. But so far they hadn't been able to locate the guy.

The Boston PD had even put a tail on Darla Hostetler and her family just in case Lenny had the nerve to seek out his ex-wife, but it had been weeks, and the Boston folks were starting to squawk. Lenny hadn't shown his nose in Massachusetts, and maybe he never would. He'd had plenty of other women on the side, women who had been contacted for information regarding Lenny. Women who had been willing enough to help, given the way things always ended when it came to Lenny—badly. Unfortunately again, none of them had been able to provide much help in finding the guy.

"A pissed-off ex-husband would at least be a motive we could work with," he told Sue.

"I heard Lenny Hostetler was maybe seen here in Rumor the day Harriet was killed."

He looked over at Sue, who shrugged innocently. "You know how gossip travels in this town, hon. It's not named Rumor for nothing. Besides, I run into Henry Raines nearly every week in the grocery store, and he's been spouting off how he saw a stranger in town that day."

For a former mayor and a practicing attorney, who happened to represent the victim, Henry Raines had a mighty big mouth, in Holt's opinion. He also had a big opinion of himself and his prowess with women, and Holt had speculated more than once about whether the divorced man had been involved with Harriet on more than a professional level.

"A stranger in town doesn't automatically equal Lenny Hostetler," Holt said.

"Yes, but I also see Louise Holmes nearly every week, too," Sue said. "She told me how Harriet had helped poor Darla Hostetler and her little ones get away to Boston."

"Yeah, well, good ol' Lenny is nowhere to be found. He might have plenty of twisted motives to want to have hurt Harriet, but we still haven't been able to place him at the scene."

Sue sighed faintly. "Harriet was an odd duck, I'll admit it. I've never seen two sisters so different as Louise and Harriet."

"Odd or not," Holt flipped open his notes, "Harriet did some good things for other people. She just wasn't as open about it as Louise. She was private. Didn't want the town knowing her business."

"Sounds like someone else I know and love," Sue said pointedly. But she was smiling slightly when Holt looked up at her.

He shook his head and started to glance back down at his notes, but a movement from across the street caught his attention through the window. The pencil he was holding snapped in two as he watched Molly skip up the front steps and unlock the entrance.

She wore a white dress with no sleeves and as she moved, the waves of her hair—not tied up in a knot for once—drifted around her bare shoulders.

Then, in the moment before she disappeared inside, she looked across the wide street, almost as if she sensed his attention. And maybe she could see him sitting there, behind the half-opened blinds of his window, for she suddenly turned and darted inside, as if the devil himself was after her.

Bold and saucy one minute. Nervous and skittish the next. Was Molly another abused wife whom Harriet had helped?

All the signs pointed that way.

It might put him closer to finding a suspect in an angry spouse. It also put every protective instinct he possessed in a meat grinder. If he had the hots for her, it was a dead bet that she would turn out to be just like Vanessa—a liar and a cheat.

Nobody deserved to be beaten on by their spouses, not even liars and cheats.

He shoved away from his desk, stuffing his little notepad in his pocket. "I'll be at the library," he told Sue.

"You might consider wiping the drool off your chin before you go over there."

He stopped in front of her desk, his eyes narrowed. "What?"

Sue's smile was all innocence, but her eyes were razor sharp with laughter. "You think I can't recognize a smitten man when I see one? Every morning I watch you watch our shy librarian walk up the steps of the library."

"I do not." His neck felt hot.

She snorted. "Hon, you look like my oldest boy used to look when we'd stop at the pet store. He could never go inside because he was allergic to everything in fur, but that boy'd press his nose up against the plate-glass window and sigh over every puppy he could see."

"Molly Brewster is a witness in Harriet's case. That's it."

"She's an available woman, who'd almost be pretty if she'd leave her hair down more often and pinch a little color into her cheeks."

"She's pretty the way she is."

Sue's smile went from sly to triumphant.

Holt turned on his heel and escaped. Well, he almost escaped. He had his hand on the door when he heard his name and turned to see Dave standing in the doorway of his office, gesturing him back.

Ignoring Sue, the formerly perfect woman, Holt went into his boss's office. Dave was already sitting behind his desk again, and even though it was only eight in the morning, there was a small pile of discarded pistachio shells sitting on the corner of his desk, along with two empty paper cups from the coffee Dave had taken to drinking by the gallon ever since murder had come visiting the small town under his watch.

Holt sat back in the metal and plastic chair in front of Dave's desk. "I hope you're not planning to send me out to Whitehorn again," he said mildly. "Yesterday's trip was nothing but wasted time and effort. The antique dealer there—once I caught up with him—said he'd never even seen the style of pen we took from Harriet's desk at the library. Tessa might be the best psychic on earth and she may well be correct that Harriet's lover gave that pen to her, but so far none of us have been able to find out who bought the pen, or from where."

"A lead's a lead," Dave muttered, brushing his hands through his hair, leaving the graying blond strands sticking out. "And this case has too few of 'em. The guy in Whitehorn was supposed to be some kind of expert on writing instruments."

Holt was glad to hear the comment, because there had been more than a few times when he and Dave had gone around the fence on Harriet's case. As far as Holt was concerned, Dave was a little too quick off the mark to pin the murder on some strange passerby. But then he'd had to remind himself that Rumor was Dave's town. The town where nothing bad ever happened.

And now it had. He knew the sheriff was getting pressure from the mayor and the town council to solve the case. It wasn't unreasonable, he supposed, that the sheriff wanted to put a bow back on his town's pristine image by blaming the crime on an outsider.

"The report on the castings I made of the tire tracks around Harriet's place hasn't come back from the FBI lab," he told him. "It's been nearly a month."

"I still don't think the tracks you found are going to be useful, but I'll make a call or two. Even if they can identify the tires, there's no sure bet we can tie them to Lenny Hostetler."

A call from the sheriff would go a helluva lot further than a call from a deputy sheriff. And Holt was reserving judgment on just what the tracks might prove. "So, what did you need? I was heading over to meet with Molly Brewster this morning."

"That'll have to wait. I've got something else for you." Dave shuffled through some of the papers on his desk, then unearthed one in particular that he pushed toward Holt. "Got a report again of rustling out at the Jupe spread."

Holt didn't want to wait. "That'll be the fourth report in as many weeks," he said. "If that idiot Jupe would just fix his downed fences, his cattle wouldn't be heading for greener pastures."

"Horton Jupe is a long-standing member of the community."

Holt tamped down his impatience. A long-standing supporter of Dave's campaign to remain sheriff was more like it. Jupe was ornery and a constant thorn in the side of those who owned land next to him.

He reminded Holt of his grandfather.

"If his fences are down, then you can just help him get them back up. You're not in Los Angeles anymore. We pitch in where we need to pitch in."

Holt rose. There hadn't been many times he'd been frustrated with the slow, uncomplicated pace of the Rumor Sheriff Department, and just about any other time, he'd have been ready to help a stubborn old coot keep his fences in place.

He'd never thought he'd see the day, but he *liked*

his life in Rumor. Just because he wasn't out rubbing elbows with everybody didn't mean he wasn't satisfied with the results of his last-ditch effort to keep his sanity by getting as far away from the kind of life he'd led as possible.

"Every day that passes means a colder trail, Dave. I'd think apprehending a murderer might take a higher priority than Horton Jupe's herd of twelve mangy cows."

"You think you're gonna find a murderer lurking in the bookshelves between civil war history and animal husbandry? Molly Brewster doesn't know squat about Harriet's private life!" The sheriff's face went redder with each rising word, making Holt wonder if the guy's blood pressure was ready to shoot off the charts. Dave was only fifty-two, but his temper had been growing increasingly short.

"Harriet spent better than fifty percent of her time in that library across the street," he said, keeping his own temper sternly in check. "Usually with Molly Brewster. She's got to know *something*, even if it is a seemingly inconsequential detail. That's how cases unravel, Dave, and you damn well know it. With one thread that happens to get pulled just right. You gave me this case, now get off my back so I can work it."

Dave glared at him. Holt stared right back. Dave was a good ol' boy. Rumor born and bred...and elected. He had the power to fire Holt if he so chose, but he didn't have a tenth of the experience Holt possessed when it came to investigating major crimes. And they both knew it.

The sheriff backed down first. "Fine." He leaned back in his desk chair and took a swipe at the empty pistachio shells. Only half of them rained into the metal trash can beside the desk; the other half scattered on the floor. "Go waste your time with the librarian, then. But you do it after you've taken care of Jupe."

So much for the sheriff backing down.

Holt left the office in disgust.

He was shoving tools in the back of his SUV when Pierce Dalton, the mayor, drove into the parking lot. Chelsea Kearns, Pierce's fiancée, was with him, and she climbed from the car the moment Pierce parked, to hurry over to Holt.

"How's the investigation?"

Holt tossed wire cutters into the toolbox he'd taken from the storage area in the back of the station. "Almost as dead as Harriet," he muttered as he slammed shut the metal box.

"Any luck in identifying the initials that Harriet wrote before she died?"

"H. I. N. or M. Maybe R. No." He lifted the heavy toolbox into the rear of his vehicle. "Between Colby and me, we've gone through county tax records, DMV, you name it. There was nobody with those initials who fit the profile you came up with. Unless we start seriously looking at females as an option, the names we found are of no use. Mayor," Holt greeted Pierce, who'd joined them.

"I know Colby is as anxious to find his aunt's murderer as anybody is," Chelsea murmured, threading her fingers through Pierce's.

"More interested than the sheriff seems to be," Holt said flatly. He looked at Pierce. "I hope you're not behind Dave wanting to sweep this business under the rug as if it never happened at all in perfect little Rumor."

Pierce's blue eyes narrowed a little. "You know me better than that."

Holt shoved his hands through his hair, getting a grip on his impatience. Pierce was a good mayor. A successful businessman. Holt respected him, and there weren't a whole lot of people he respected.

"You look like you're preparing to build a barn," Chelsea said, obviously wanting to lighten the tension that hummed between the men.

"Building Horton Jupe's fences, more like," Holt corrected. "He's called in another complaint of rustling."

Pierce made a face. "Not to underestimate the seriousness of that particular crime, but no rustler worth his salt would take even one of Jupe's scrawny moos."

"Well, I know that, and you know that." Holt closed the tailgate with a slam. "The sheriff, however, wants me to go out there and fix some fence and calm the man down. Seeing how the case is such a priority over other things going on."

Pierce looked resigned. "I'll talk to Dave." He brushed his hand gently over Chelsea's auburn head then headed off for the building.

The mayor could talk all he wanted, it didn't mean the sheriff's stance was likely to change. Dave Reingard had been sheriff for so long that his ways were set in stone.

"Chelsea, are you sure there's no evidence on Harriet to tie Lenny Hostetler to this?"

"I wish there was." Her green eyes were sad. "But you know as much as I know, Holt. Harriet's place was spotless. Before the shot that killed her, she was struck with a blunt object on the back of her head near the neck. An object we couldn't find, or even identify based on the wound. There weren't even any fingerprints we could lift from Harriet herself. No fibers, no defensive wounds, nothing except a bruise on her hip that matched the chair-rail molding in her house, strongly suggesting she'd been pushed hard against the wall. That was it—the bruise, the trauma to her neck and the single shot to her head by a weapon registered to her.''

Holt looked beyond Chelsea to the library across the street. ''And there's no good explanation for why Harriet had that gun at all. Did you know that her tax records indicated a substantial donation last year to an avid gun-control group?''

''The registration for the gun seemed perfectly straightforward.''

''Maybe so,'' he murmured. ''But *why* did she have the thing in the first place? There was even that empty drawer in her sideboard at her place that was specially lined with fabric, perfectly fitted to hold the weapon, when all the drawers around it held a half-ton of little odds and ends. The whole thing seems strange to me.''

''Maybe the weapon was a gift.''

''Like the gold pen was a gift?'' Holt shoved back his hair. He needed a haircut but hadn't managed to find the time to fit it in. ''I know Tessa Madison had some sort of vision or something when she touched Harriet's pen that told her it had been given to Harriet by her lover.''

''Tessa never touched the gun?''

Holt shook his head. ''It's in the evidence locker, and the sheriff would have blown a gasket if we'd given her access to it. She never went into Harriet's house, either. It's still sealed.''

''Harriet's house hadn't been ransacked,'' Chelsea murmured. ''Whoever shot her either knew where the gun was kept, or she already had it out for some reason only to end up having it used against her.''

''If she were afraid that Lenny Hostetler was coming after her, she might have the gun at her side. It would be his style to bang her around a bit first. But if she were afraid of some sort of attack—enough that she was keeping her weapon out in the open instead of in that little drawer—why didn't she just call it in to the sheriff department?'' Again Holt dragged his fingers through his hair. ''Circles. We're going around in circles and it's driving me nuts.''

Chelsea smiled softly and patted his arm. ''Have patience. You'll figure it out, Holt.''

She excused herself then, and Holt watched her walk toward the buildings. Pierce Dalton's office was located in the building right next to the sheriff's department, and she was becoming a pretty familiar face over there since she'd gotten engaged to the mayor.

Holt thought he might have an invitation to their wedding sitting somewhere on his desk in the station, but couldn't swear to it. He vaguely recalled that the ceremony was supposed to be held outside the Blue Spruce, the resort that Dalton owned.

''Figure it out.'' He shook his head and climbed into the SUV. ''Yeah, while I'm out stapling barbwire to fence posts.''

Driving out of the parking lot, he double-parked in front of the library and strode up the steps. He found Molly sitting on the floor in the carpeted children's section, surrounded by a half dozen little kids.

Every single one of them was leaning toward her, faces rapt. And Molly, God in heaven, was smiling as she held up a picture book and read aloud to her miniature audience.

Off to the side, where she hadn't yet noticed him, his feet forgot how to walk, apparently, and he stood there, rooted to the floor. One part of his mind jeered at him for acting just as fascinated as the kids. The rest of him was too busy memorizing the curving, joyful tilt of her pink lips, the dancing in her sky-blue eyes, to care.

The kids might be fascinated with the tale of a pint-size girl who was hot on the trail of a thief, but Molly could have been reading a label from a can of dog food and he wouldn't have minded.

As long as she kept that smile on her face.

Then, as if she heard his thoughts or something, her gaze shifted and she looked right at him.

The book in her hand wavered. Not a lot, not enough for the children to notice. But for him it was more than plenty. The shining in her eyes dimmed, and though she kept the smile on her face, he figured it was only because she pinned it there through sheer effort. Because the joy had definitely oozed out of it.

Familiar territory, he thought, his feet unrooting from the floor as he walked over to her. Her expression wasn't *quite* filled with loathing, but there was definitely no pleasure there.

He was a bloody idiot for letting that bug him, too. Loathing or smiling, Molly Brewster and her secrets were only part of the Martel investigation; they were nothing else to him, at all. Nothing.

"Deputy Tanner." She spoke first, and he suddenly found himself the focus of several pairs of curious young eyes. "Is there something I can do for you?"

Several suggestions sprang to mind, and none of them were suitable for their underage audience. "I'm sorry to interrupt." He could be polite if he had to. "But I wanted to let you know that I wouldn't be here this morning like I'd—" warned "—told you."

"Did you come to arrest Miss Molly?"

Holt and Molly both stared at the boy who'd spoken.

"Of course not, Nathaniel," Molly said, and Holt had to give her credit for keeping her voice smooth— filled with humor, actually.

"My mom said Dep'ty Tanner does a lot of arresting." Nathaniel was looking superior, now that he had the fascinated attention of his peers.

Holt looked more closely at the freckle-faced boy. "Are you Dennis Jones's boy?"

Nathaniel nodded. "And my mom says you got a lotta nerve. More nerve 'n Sheriff Reingard's got, 'cause he always leaves my pa alone when he's not feeling real good."

Since Holt had arrested Dennis Jones three times in eight months for being drunk and disorderly against the shrill protests of his skinny wife, he imagined that the woman did have plenty to say about him. But Jones's "not feeling real good" had led to him busting up his favorite bar out toward the highway.

Every time Jones took a drink, he also used a bar stool on the place, never hurting anyone but always doing plenty of property damage, which he'd later write a check to cover. Jones was another favored donor to Sheriff Reingard's past campaigns for re-election.

Molly was looking distinctly uncomfortable. "The deputy is a man we can go to for *help*," she said. "That's what the police or the sheriff's department are there for. To protect everyone. To help us when we need help. Now here," she took three books that had been sitting on the floor beside her and set them out in front of the small group. "You look through these and decide what we'll read next time, and I'll be right back."

Holt held out his hand, and with six young witnesses there was nothing for Molly to do but take it. As soon as she was standing, though, she tugged her hand free and made a production of brushing down the long folds of her dress that had been tucked around her legs.

Well, why not? She probably figured she needed to wipe off the germs from touching the likes of him. Holt leaned over a little. "Bet it nearly killed you to say those good things about us law enforcement types."

She huffed and walked several feet away from the children. "I don't appreciate you interrupting me this way," she said when he joined her.

"I could have let you sit and stew all day wondering when I'd finally show up again. Is that what you'd prefer?"

She tilted her head a little, the curve of her smooth jaw tightening. "What I'd *prefer* is that you leave me alone entirely, but you already know that and have chosen to harass me anyway."

"Harass?" He carefully kept his voice lowered.

"I don't think so. But you're free to make your complaints to the sheriff if you feel so inclined."

"Right." Her lips twisted. "I know how it really works. All of you stand together no matter what."

Holt pinched the bridge of his nose. It was too early in the day for a headache, but damned if one wasn't merrily forming. "My former co-workers would be delighted to tell you how wrong you are on that point." His voice was dark, his mood going even darker. "How many of these junior soirées do you have today?"

"Oh, now you're concerned about interrupting my schedule?" She looked over at the children, who were more interested in watching them than selecting their next storybook, and pasted the smile back on her face. "It didn't seem to bother you last night when you were tossing about your orders for me to be available to help you."

She was right, and his thorough aggravation with the entire day grew just a bit more. "How many?"

"Just this morning group today." Her voice wasn't quite grudging, but it was close.

"So, if I come back this afternoon, we can get some work done on Harriet's case."

"Don't speak as if you're leaving me any kind of choice."

Holt exhaled wearily. Her dress wasn't completely white, he noticed. There were tiny little blue flowers sewn into the thin, delicate-looking fabric along the neckline that ran nearly straight from one slender shoulder across to the other. "Molly, there is always a choice."

"Sure. Between one devil or another." Without looking at him, she returned to the children and sank down onto the floor again, her skirt drifting around her ankles like a white cloud.

She was smiling again, but he couldn't see any of that natural happiness in it.

Feeling like the devil she'd accused him of being, and hating it, he walked away.

Chapter Six

It was the laughter that caught Holt's attention as he
stood in the crowd of people awaiting a seat in the
jam-packed Calico Diner.

He almost expected to see her before he even
looked toward the source of that lilting laugh. And
sure enough, there was Molly Brewster, sitting by
herself in one of the red vinyl booths. Standing beside the table was Callie Sullivan, the owner of the
old-fashioned diner, who looked as if she was taking
Molly's order.

It was noisy and boisterous, particularly where he
stood, behind a large family with three kids who
were currently arguing over a handheld game. But
Holt still heard that laughter, and it went straight to
his gut with all the precision of a laser.

He'd spent the entire day out at Horton Jupe's
spread. His back ached from digging postholes, and

his butt ached from sitting in a saddle. Even after a shower and a change of clothes, he was hot, tired and hungry.

Once again he'd never made it to the library to thoroughly pick Molly Brewster's brain.

As he continued to wait in line, he watched Molly. Nobody came to join her in that small booth. She smiled and nodded at a lot of the folks who passed by or hailed greetings from their own seats, but the bench across from her remained empty.

The family in front of Holt moved off when Callie summoned them to a large circular table, and Holt watched them, deliberately keeping his attention from Molly at the other end of the diner. The youths were still arguing over the game, and with a loud voice that drew several startled gazes from the people eating, the father took it away from all of them.

After settling the family, Callie returned and stopped in front of Holt. Her long, blond hair was pulled back in a typical ponytail, and her blue eyes were bright.

"Hey, there, Mr. Lawman," she greeted him with a quick hug. Callie was just like that. As friendly and generous as a woman could be. She was married to Nick Sullivan, who was the president of the Rumor Chamber of Commerce, and there was not a single hint of mystery about her. "I'm sorry for the wait." She ran a practiced eye over the diner. "It's going to be a while longer, too, I'm afraid. I can't believe how busy we are tonight."

"Nobody wants to stay home and cook when it's still so hot outside."

"Well," Callie said humorously, "it's cooking inside here with all these bodies. I can bring you something to drink while you wait if you'd like. We've got a few people at the counter who've just gotten their entrée. They'll likely be the first ones out of here to free up a seat for you.''

There already was a free seat.

Right across from Molly Brewster.

''Think I'll join that lady right over there,'' he told Callie. ''And to make it even easier, you can throw in an order for iced tea for me and whatever your special is tonight.''

Callie looked over her shoulder, then back at Holt. ''You be nice to Molly,'' she warned softly.

''Me? I'm always nice.''

''No, you're always thorough. I've seen you wipe the floor at Nick's poker games too many times to fall for the 'nice' routine.''

''Poker is one thing. Dinner another. Besides, if you want to lecture someone on good behavior at the dinner table, you can visit that table you just seated.'' Holt glanced over when another burst of raised voices drew attention.

Callie whistled silently. ''Might be glad we've got you here this evening for more than the business you're giving me, even if you are off duty. I'll bring your tea right out.''

''Thanks.'' Holt headed toward Molly's table. It was stupid, but it seemed like a long walk over to that small booth in the back of the trailer-shaped diner. And it seemed as if every eye in the place watched him take that long walk.

Except Molly, whose nose was buried in a book as she tucked the straw of a strawberry malt between her lips. It must be a thick malt, he thought, watching her cheeks hollow out a little as she sucked on the straw.

He abruptly slid into the booth, and her head jerked up. "You've got that deer-in-the-headlights look," he said softly.

"What are you d-doing here?"

"Taking the only available seat in the place. Do you mind?"

"Would it matter if I did?"

Too damn much. "Nope."

Callie breezed by, a whirl of motion, as she set the tea in front of him and went on to another table and began unloading salads from the heavy tray she wielded. He lifted the glass, drinking thirstily.

"Your nose is sunburned." Molly looked as if she regretted making the observation, considering the way she was staring into her malt again.

"Spent the day outside."

"You needed sunblock."

"Nice to know you're concerned." He shook some sugar into the tea and stirred it.

Her lips tightened and her eyes flashed a quick glance at him. "I'm not. I was just grateful for the reprieve, since you were obviously too busy to come by the library and ruin my afternoon, too. But now, I suppose you're intent on ruining my dinner."

He almost felt like smiling. He far preferred the Molly with some fight in her to the Molly who looked as if a raised word would shatter her.

Problem was, he liked all of the Mollys a little too much. And watching the way she drank her malt— soft lips pursed around the end of the straw that she sort of rolled back and forth between her thumb and forefinger—was maddening.

"I'm too hungry to want to ruin anybody's meal."
The self-deprecating humor was lost on her. Thank-
fully. If she knew how he reacted just from watching
her toy with that straw of hers, she'd rightfully race
for the hills. So he focused on the more obvious is-
sue. "I'm off duty and I won't mention Harriet's
case if you won't. What's the word on your car? I
saw it sitting at the garage with a half dozen others
in front of it."

She blinked. "Um. The fan belt was an easy fix.
But the alternator is going to take a little longer. It
broke down right there when I was trying to drive it
home. They have to order parts, I guess, because it's
so old."

"Speaking of old, you ever met Horton Jupe?"

Again she hesitated, probably searching for some
ulterior motive in his questions. "He comes into the
library every week," she finally said. "Reads Louis
L'Amour. Avidly."

"Too bad he doesn't read *Ranching for Idiots*."

A huff of laughter escaped her lips, and she
clamped a hand over her mouth, her translucent eyes
peeping over her fingers. Her expression would have
been guilty except for the sparkle of amusement in
them. And just that easily, Holt forgot the miserable,
frustrating way he'd spent the entire day.

He was a bad case.

"I was out at his place all day. Fixing his fences
and trying to convince him that nobody's trying to
rustle his herd."

"Um, you mean *helping* him to fix his fences,
don't you?"

"No. I mean fixing them. Jupe sat in the back of
his pickup truck on a striped, cushioned chair with a

gold-fringed awning overhead that he claims came from France a hundred years ago.''

Molly eyed the deputy, not certain if he was joking or not. His expression certainly looked serious enough. But then, Holt Tanner's serious expression rarely changed, as far as she could tell. She knew he had a sense of humor, but there was little humor to be found in the reason why he kept intruding in her quiet life. ''I'm sure Mr. Jupe was very grateful for the assistance.''

''Even if it did come from me, you mean? Jupe swore a blue streak over my head every thirty minutes. I think it was mostly to remind me that he was still alive under that umbrella that put the 'ug' in ugly, but I suppose it might have been his gratitude showing.''

Molly dragged her eyes from the way the deputy's lip had curled up at the corner. ''I don't believe he was really swearing at you.''

''Well, he was. Reminded me of my grandfather.''

''The one who had the place near Billings.''

He nodded. His eyes were as dark as tree bark when his gaze settled on her face. Molly's cheeks heated, and she quickly ducked her head over her straw, telling herself harshly that the man had *not* been looking at her mouth.

But a person could only drink down so much malted milk without getting a brain freeze, and she finally had to look back up.

He was still watching her, only now there was a muscle ticking rhythmically in his angled jaw, making it look even more sharp and hard despite the faint blurring of a five-o'clock shadow.

She swallowed. The man gave *tall, dark and handsome* new meaning. She'd thought so the very first time she'd seen him in Rumor. And then she'd learned he was the deputy sheriff, and she'd deliberately put his appeal right out of her mind. Or so she'd thought. "Deputy, I—"

"Holt. We're just sharing a dinner table, Molly."

"Really. You wouldn't be anywhere near me if it weren't for Harriet's murder."

His gaze was steady. "Are you so sure about that?"

Breathless. He made her breathless.

It *had* to be nerves. It had to be!

"Here you go." Callie appeared beside them and began sliding plates onto the table. When she left, Molly just stared at the food.

"Molly." His voice was soft. "Eat."

She couldn't. Her heart was thundering, her throat too tight to speak, to do more than draw in a tight, squeaking breath. What on earth was *wrong* with her?

And then she heard a crash of dishes, and yelling erupted from across the diner. The family with the three kids that had been standing in front of Holt in line. Molly had seen them all come in, and had kept her eyes on her book. As if by pretending to be invisible, maybe Holt wouldn't see her sitting there by herself and take advantage of the situation to probe her knowledge of Harriet.

She was vaguely aware of Holt looking at her as she stared over at the family, unable to drag her gaze away no matter how badly she wanted to. The father had shoved back his chair and was towering over his family, his voice loud and angry.

Across from her, Holt muttered something unrepeatable, and slid out of the booth, heading over to the commotion.

Just as the father grabbed one of the boys by the arm and yanked him from his seat, Molly darted from the booth and raced outside, not waiting to see what Holt would do, not wanting to see a second more.

Sucking in gulps of the humid night air, she simply kept moving, kept running until the rocking in her stomach finally, finally began to settle.

Only then did she look up. Only then did she catch her breath, pressing her hand to the stitch in her side, and pay the slightest heed to where she'd ended up.

She was in the park.

And it was dark, barely lit by the occasional streetlight over near the playground. But at least it was silent. Nobody yelling, nobody crying.

Except her.

She swiped her cheeks and sat down right there on the grassy field between the lake and the playground, uncaring even when the automatic sprinklers suddenly kicked on, raining over her. She hugged her arms around her drawn-up legs and pressed her forehead to her knees.

"You are in control," she whispered the words aloud. Then repeated them. And again.

But it was futile. Because she wasn't. She wasn't in control, and ever since Harriet's murder, that fact had become increasingly obvious to her. She was jumpier, more nerve-racked now, than she had been a year ago when every unexpected noise had her envisioning Rob around the nearest corner, still watching her every move.

"Molly."

She jerked, peering at Holt through the spray of water surrounding her. The droplets caught the lights from the ball field and they looked like jewels as they danced through the night. She covered her forehead and eyes with her hand. "Go away."

"It's a public park."

"Fine. Don't go away. But leave me alone." The words ought to have been tart. It killed her that they sounded thick with tears. Not even when Rob had been at his worst had she been driven to tears. Fear. Desperation. But not tears. She'd simply refused to give him that power over her, not when he'd already taken so much away from her. Since Harriet's murder, though, tears had been coming far too easily.

"You know I can't do that."

"Yes, because I'm some dangerous criminal type who shouldn't be trusted. Now you can really do something about it, because I forgot to leave money for the bill!"

She stiffened when he walked through the sprinklers toward her. He was holding something out, but not until he got nearer did she realize it was her small purse.

"The bill is taken care of. You forgot this at the diner."

She snatched it from him and dropped it on the grass beside her. "Taken care of by whom?" Please don't let it be *him*.

"Callie. She knows you're good for it."

Molly frowned. She *was*. "Okay, so you've brought me my purse. You've done your public service, why don't you go arrest somebody. That father in there might be a good start."

"He and his wife are having dinner at the Rooftop

Café," Holt told her. "Their three kids are with D.J. Reingard and a bunch of his friends at somebody's barbecue birthday party. Somebody named Tiffany, I think."

Molly watched with dismay when he slowly lowered himself to the ground beside her.

"Spent too much time in the saddle today," he muttered as he stretched out his jean-clad legs. "I'm more used to a Harley than a quarter horse these days." He tilted his head back a little, not even bothering to brush the water drops from his face as they fell on him.

He confused her. He confounded her. And just then she wasn't sure what else he made her feel. Only that whatever it was, she wasn't sure she liked it. "What are you doing, Deputy Tanner?"

"Holt," he said. "This town hardly stands on ceremony, Molly. You've lived here twice as long as I have, surely you've noticed it. Might as well try the name. It may be a four-letter word, but it's nothing you'll get your mouth washed out for saying. Not by me, anyway. Holt. You didn't seem to have a problem with it that day we first met. You remember?"

In the hardware aisle at the general store. She'd been choosing lightbulbs and he'd been selecting a hammer. They'd accidentally backed into each other, and his hammer had made mincemeat of her extralong-life outdoor bulb. And his mobile mouth had tilted at the corner as he stuck out his hand and offered his first name.

Two minutes after their collision, her undeniable breathlessness with the handsome man had died a hasty death when the clerk had rounded the corner with a broom and greeted the black-haired stranger as "Deputy." Molly had grabbed a different light-bulb and scurried away.

"*Holt,*" she said now, cheeks burning. "What are you doing? Isn't it bad enough that people are going to think I've lost my mind, but you want them think-ing that about you, too?"

"I think maybe you're the sensible one." He lay right on his back, arms folded behind his head, legs crossed at the ankles, looking as comfortable as if he were lying out on a beach in California, soaking up the sun instead of water sprayed from a sprinkler. "More of this town oughta come out and sit in the sprinklers for a while. Pretty good idea you had, Molly."

Definitely confused her. "You're insane."

"You know what they say. It's the ones who are sure they're sane that aren't."

She looked down at him lying there on the grass, water making his gray T-shirt look dark and his black hair even blacker. "Well," she said faintly, "it's the coolest I've been in weeks."

"Nick Sullivan and Pierce Dalton are planning some sort of cooling-off celebration here in the park at the end of the month," he said. "I wonder if we can talk them into doing it with the sprinklers run-ning, 'cause I really think you're on to something here."

She pushed her wet hair away from her face. "This is the strangest conversation I've ever had in my life. Nothing's normal with you."

"What's normal?" He rolled on his side facing her and propped his head on his hand. "That family in the Calico tonight? They'd been on the road for nearly thirty-two hours. Driving in a car with no air-conditioning from Maine to Seattle for a funeral at the end of the week. That wasn't normal for them.''

''So somebody had the bright idea of giving them some time away from each other.''

''The kids will get some of that built-up energy out of their systems, and their parents will have a few hours of peace with each other before they have to set off again and deal with the changes life has tossed at them.''

''It was *your* idea,'' she realized.

''Even guys with four-letter names can come up with a helpful idea now and again.''

Molly had to look away from his steady gaze. It saw entirely too much. Her fingers began plucking at the folds of her dress that tangled about her ankles. She wasn't thoroughly wet yet, but she was getting there.

Holt rolled onto his back again. And the only sounds they heard were the crickets chirping and the rhythmic tick-tick-tick-tick-*whoosh* of the sprinklers.

It was impossibly soothing. And impossible to believe that she found it just that, considering who was sharing the wet, grassy field with her.

''You want to talk about it?''

She tightened her arms a little around her legs, then made herself relax again. ''No.''

She heard him sigh. ''But you have talked about it. At least to…someone. People don't have panic attacks for no reason.''

She frowned a little, rubbing her wet cheek against her arm. ''No.''

At that he jackknifed upward. ''No? What about—''

Her eyebrows rose. ''What about *what?*''

His hair, weighted with water, fell over his fore-head and he slicked it back. "Never mind. Molly, do you know Lenny Hostetler?"

"No."

"Come on, think about it, at least. If you don't know him personally, maybe you've heard the name. Lenny Hostetler. Or Darla Hostetler."

"I don't need to think about it. I don't know either one personally, and I've never heard the name. Either name. Why?"

He shook his head a little. "Just looking for a thread," he said, sounding frustrated.

It didn't take a genius to know he was thinking about Harriet's case. Molly plucked at her skirt again. She picked several blades of cut grass from her toes and smoothed down the edge of the adhesive strip on her shin that was working loose. She swallowed, and prayed she wasn't making the biggest mistake of her life. "I think Harriet *did* keep a diary."

Holt remained silent, but she knew his attention was thoroughly and completely focused on her. She knew it, because she could feel it right down to her toes. Only instead of making her cold with fear, it made her feel…okay.

Maybe even better than okay.

The thought was almost more terrifying than simply fearing what would happen when, *if*, he ran that fingerprint he'd taken from her glass.

She moistened her lips. They'd had a deal. He wouldn't use the print and she'd help him understand Harriet's life. She had to believe that he would stick by his word. Despite him being a cop, she had to believe that everything she'd given up hadn't been for naught. She had to believe it, or simply lose her mind.

"You know the gold pen you took from her office?" She didn't wait for his nod. "It was a gift to Harriet. She never said from whom, but I remember when she received it. I don't know, about six months ago now, maybe. For the longest time she even kept the wrapping paper from the package folded inside her desk drawer, along with the ribbons. Blue wrapping. The foil kind. Shiny. Thin, white, curled ribbons. She, uh, she mentioned once that she kept the pen with her journal. That's what she called it. A journal. Not a diary. And the pen was the only one she used to write in it."

"But the journal wasn't with the pen in her office at the library."

She shot him a quick look.

"I'm not accusing anything, Molly. Just stating a fact. We practically tore apart her office looking for evidence. No journal. No tenderly saved wrapping paper or curly ribbons, no little love notes, no cards, no messages."

"She threw away the wrapping paper and ribbons shortly before she died."

"How shortly?"

"I don't know. A week. Maybe two. I saw it in her trash can one afternoon, that's the only reason I knew about it. We were having a meeting in her office. Me, Harriet, the regular volunteers who work the circulation desk, we were all crammed into Harriet's office, talking about the new computer system. Harriet hated computers, you know. She said—"

"—they were sucking the intelligence out of our

kids,'' Holt finished. ''I heard her say that once when I was in the library.''

''Right. That's right. She really loathed the things, but really I think she was just afraid of not knowing how to use one for anything other than hooking into the interlibrary system.'' Molly knew she was talking too much. Rambling too much. But she just couldn't seem to make herself stop, now that she'd begun. ''I didn't make a habit of rooting through her desk,'' she continued. ''Harriet…Harriet was a very private person.''

''Why did you keep quiet about the journal when I've been asking you from the beginning if you knew of one?''

Molly knew enough to expect the question. But even then, hearing it voiced, knowing it was more than justified, she wanted to bury her head.

But Harriet had been killed. She deserved so much more than Molly's cowardice.

Her vision blurred. ''Because,'' her voice was barely a whisper, ''I was afraid of what Harriet might have written in it. About me.''

Chapter Seven

Holt's gut tightened. He'd known it. Molly had been too secretive from the get-go. And he'd been too damned aware of her, his senses nearly rocketing off the chart whenever he saw her. Hell, whenever he thought of her.

"We've gotta do this at the station," he said, his voice sounding oddly rusty. "You can call an attorney first, if you want, or we'll arrange one for you."

The breath she sucked in was audible in the silence that filled the air when the sprinklers abruptly quit, the spray of water going suddenly from a fine spray to a halfhearted little spurt to nothing at all.

"Why would I need an attorney?" Her voice was hushed, and so full of wariness that he would have hurt inside from it, if he'd still believed in that kind of thing.

"So that you don't say something that can later be used against you."

She scrambled to her feet, slipping a little in the slick grass. "*What?* Are you planning to arrest me or something? For what? You *said* you believed I had nothing to do with Harriet's death!"

He stood, more slowly than she, feeling the ache of his long day in every screaming joint he possessed. "Molly—"

"I'm not *hiding* the journal." Her voice was hoarse. "I didn't take it—didn't destroy it. I've never even *seen* it. All I'm telling you is that I think one does—or did—exist."

The irony was that he wanted to believe her. She'd admitted to an assumed name and now, weeks after the fact, to the existence of a personal journal kept by the victim. And still, when Holt looked into Molly Brewster's face, into those eyes that looked translucent even in the dim light of the town park, he wanted to believe every word that came out of her soft, pink lips.

Had he learned nothing from Vanessa?

He scrubbed his hands down his face, swiping at the water that still clung there, though it was already beginning to dry, thanks to the heat that didn't even abate at night.

He really was an idiot of monumental proportions.

"Come on," he said to her.

Panic rolled off her in waves. "What are you going to do?"

"Take an official statement."

"You, uh, you can't."

"Really. And why is that, Molly? Or whatever your real name is."

She looked away. "It…is my name. My, um, my middle name." Her voice shook.

"And Brewster?" He steeled himself when she faced him. Maybe her torment was real, or maybe she was just a very good actress and he should have run that fingerprint immediately instead of proving yet again that his judgment when it came to women stunk.

"Holt, please." Her hands lifted.

He wrapped his fingers around her wrist. The bones felt delicate, fragile. Oh, yeah. His judgment stunk. "Let's go."

She hung back. "I'm soaking wet. C-can I change first?"

"And give you an opportunity to skip? I don't think so."

"I wasn't—" She twisted her hand, but he held fast. "You can come with me, then, if you think I'm such a risk."

He ignored her words and began walking toward the street. He could hear her hiccupping breaths and felt like the worst kind of human being on the planet as he inexorably dragged her along with him.

They made it to the sidewalk and he stopped, glancing at her before stepping into the street. Except the glance turned into a stare, and he shook his head, muttering an oath. The streetlights showed what the darkness hadn't.

Molly's white dress wasn't merely wet; it was practically transparent. He could even see the design in the lace of her bra. Flowers. And through that flowery lace, he could see the pale shadow of her tightly drawn nipples.

A shout and a laugh from across the street seemed

to mock him. To get to the station, they'd have to walk past the Calico, the Rooftop Café and the general store, where three teenaged boys were sitting on the bench in front of the wooden Old-West-style front, looking as if they were practicing to be like eighty-year-old Barney Schoemaker, sitting in a storefront. The only thing they were missing was a game of checkers balanced on a barrel between them.

"Fine," he said abruptly, "you can change your clothes first."

Her shoulders sagged. "Thank you."

"But I'm going with you. Take it or leave it," he said when she looked set to protest. "Otherwise, we can parade you right down to the station and give everybody a thrill."

She looked down when he jerked his chin at her. Her gasp was soft, but enough to make the hair on the back of his neck prickle. She immediately folded her arms across her chest, defensiveness shrieking silently from her. It didn't abate one iota as they walked the few blocks to her little house. She didn't speak the entire time.

The drapes of her front window were drawn, but he could see the glow around them of a light she'd left burning inside. "You didn't leave on your porch light."

"I d-did. Must have burned out." He could actually hear her teeth chattering. He'd expected that her nervousness would have subsided, a little at the very least, during the walk. No such luck.

They climbed the porch steps, and she dropped first her purse, then her keys. If she *was* acting, she was the best damned actress he'd ever seen.

He leaned over and picked up the keys from the

porch, jiggling them flat on the palm of his hand. There was no cute engraved key chain, no sentimental photo encased in hard plastic. Nothing but a thin metal ring holding three keys. One key for her car, one for her house, one for the library.

A monumental fool with monumental bad judgment. The accusation sat hard in his brain. He held out his palm, anyway, and wondered when the hell he'd gotten the notion that he wanted entrance into her home by invitation, rather than coercion. "I'll wait out here."

Her brows drew together as if she were trying to decipher his reasoning. Considering *he* couldn't, he doubted she'd have any success at it. But he waited, palm flat until slowly, like some wary little squirrel seeking an acorn under the eye of a wolf, she reached for the keys and plucked them from his hand.

He walked back down the steps until he was standing in the middle of her tidy little yard. "Don't be long," he warned. "You've got five minutes, or I'm coming in."

She nodded jerkily and turned to the door.

Only to fall back a moment later with a startled cry that made his adrenaline nearly shoot through the roof. She darted down the stairs even as he was heading toward her. He caught her just as she plowed into him. Her hands scrabbled at his T-shirt. "The door."

He closed his fingers over her shoulders, nudging her back so he could see her face. "What?"

"The door isn't latched."

And that was enough to make this woman, who pretty much detested him, cling like a limpet. He looked at the house again. Not as a man who wanted a woman's invitation.

But as a cop.

An off-duty cop with nothing on him but his clothes. Of all times to leave his cell phone on his dresser at home. "Are you sure you locked it? Positive?"

She nodded. Her lips were pressed together so tightly they were white.

"Go to the neighbors," he told her, nudging her in that direction. "Call the sheriff."

Molly shook her head frantically. She wanted to scream, she wanted to hide. But she didn't want to leave Holt. He didn't trust her, and he was pure danger to her peace of mind. But she didn't fear him the way she feared the past.

"Molly, *go* to the neighbors."

"He might be over there," she pushed the words out through the vise that had become her throat.

"Who?"

"Rob." She felt sick with the seesaw of emotions rocketing her. "He did it before. Left my house opened. Made sure I knew he'd gotten in. And when I went to my next-door neighbor to c-call the police," she nearly choked on the word, "he was already there."

Hot tears burned behind her eyes as she remembered. There he'd been. Sitting on the couch alongside old Mrs. Mueller, his smile slick and cold. And triumphant when Molly had resigned herself to the fruitlessness of calling the police.

They'd never helped her before that night. There was no reason to believe they'd help her then. And when Mrs. Mueller had kindly invited Molly in to have coffee and cookies, Molly had had to sit there choking down both, afraid to leave the old woman alone with Rob. Knowing it was exactly what he'd wanted, what he'd manipulated.

"Rob," Holt repeated. His expression was fierce, and his hands on her shoulders were hard. But his voice was soft. Calm. And maybe that was what helped her say the rest.

"Thompson," she managed. "Rob Thompson. My ex-husband."

She withstood Holt's narrow-eyed inspection. "So help me, Molly, if you're lying—"

"I'm not. I've never lied to you."

"Right."

"I haven't. Not...not outright." It was one of the few things that helped her sleep at night.

He blew out a short breath and looked at the house. "Stay behind me, then. And if I tell you to stay put, you stay put. I mean it. Understand?"

She nodded, so grateful not to have to go next door that she would have agreed to just about anything right then. Maybe she was being supremely paranoid, but she'd graduated paranoia cum laude courtesy of a lunatic.

Holt didn't go straight to the front door as she might have expected. He walked quietly around the entire house, studying the windows, looking at the ground beneath them. And at the back door he silently pointed at her, waiting until she stood still before he went up and tried the door.

It was locked.

They went up the other side of the house and again he checked every single window. And around to the front once more. Where the porch light was burned out and the lamp in her living room glowed around the sides of the draperies hanging over the big picture window.

"Are you sure you locked it?"

"Yes."

"There's no sign of anything else being disturbed."

She stared at the front of her house. It had been her haven for a year and a half. If Rob had somehow found her, what was the house now?

"That's what he'd do. Make it look like I was crazy to everyone else, while letting me know that he could get to me anytime he chose."

"Whoever it was, if anyone, is probably long gone," Holt said. "But I'm gonna go in and check it out. If you won't go to your neighbor, then stay on the sidewalk."

She didn't want to be left alone. But she didn't want to go in her house. Not if Rob had truly been there.

Damned if she did, damned if she didn't.

It was a familiar place for her, and she loathed it as much as she ever had.

Her wet dress clung uncomfortably to her legs, the refreshment it had provided earlier long gone. She was shivering, and it was a conscious effort to keep her teeth from chattering as she watched Holt silently enter her house.

She'd never voluntarily allowed a man entry into this house. And now, of all people, she was absurdly grateful that Holt was the one entering.

What on God's green earth was wrong with her?

He was back out in minutes, though it seemed eons. He walked straight over to her. "It's clear. Sheriff's on his way. I called from inside. Come on.

You're gonna have to tell me if anything is missing or disturbed inside.''

He touched her arm when she just stood there on the sidewalk. ''You don't have to stay there tonight,'' he added, almost seeming to read her mind. ''But you've got to go through it enough so we can make the report. And you need dry clothes. You're shivering.''

She knew he was right. About the clothes at least. She wasn't sure what she would do about an alternative roof over her head, though. So she did what she could manage.

Putting one foot in front of the other, concentrating on just that, took her up to the door. Holt stayed by her side right into the living room. ''Don't touch anything,'' he said. ''Just let me know if there is anything missing.''

She ran her eyes over the room. ''There won't be anything missing,'' she whispered. ''My book is moved.''

''Which one?''

She moistened her lips and crossed to the bookshelf. There was one hardcover that was lying on its side in front of the others that were neatly standing, spines out. ''This one.'' She pointed, but didn't touch it. Rob would never be stupid enough to leave fingerprints, though.

Holt looked at the title. ''*How to Take Control of Your Life—and Keep It.* Where was it moved from?''

''The coffee table.'' From outside she could hear a lone siren. She headed down the hall to the opened doorway of the one bedroom the small house possessed. She looked inside, feeling ill. Holt came up behind her, and she turned away from her bedroom, her eyes stinging.

"Molly. What is it?"

"It's starting all over again."

He made a rough sound, cupping her shoulders. "I'm not going to let anything happen to you." His voice was low. "But you've gotta let me in enough to know what we're dealing with."

"He rearranged the pillows on my bed."

Holt looked from her pale face to her bedroom through the doorway. The bed looked painfully small in comparison to the king he had taking up nearly all the floor space in his apartment bedroom. She had a white bedspread, the short kind that only reached partway down the sides, a white skirt around the bottom, and a half dozen white pillows of varying sizes stacked neatly at the head of the bed.

It looked like something out of a catalog, he thought. It also looked innocent. Hell, the bed looked positively virginal.

"How can you tell they've been rearranged?" His bed had only two pillows. And they were getting so flat that he had to bunch one of 'em up under his head to make it even useful.

"The embroidered one is in the center. The rest all squared up."

"So?"

"So, I don't arrange them that way! All orderly and lunatic looking." She turned and took half a dozen steps toward the bathroom. She didn't even look inside as she threw out her arm, pointing. "Look at the towels hanging on the bar. They'll be folded in fourths. Four on the bar. The short ones on the outside, long ones on the inside."

The back of his neck prickled again. He looked past her into the bathroom. There was nothing fancy about the small room, plain white tile, plain white porcelain, but it was sparkling clean and nearly sterile in its orderliness. He could even smell the faint odor of disinfectant along with the flowery smell of the fresh cake of soap sitting on a ceramic soap dish. The only color in the room came from the deep-blue towels hanging on the towel bar in just the manner she'd described.

"The closet'll be rearranged in the bedroom, too." Her voice was nearly hoarse, and she about jumped out of her skin when they both heard the heavy footsteps behind them.

The sheriff was standing at the end of the hall.

"I'm gonna have to take the stuff you say he touched," Holt warned Molly. "At least the towels and pillows. Okay?"

Her nod was faint. She *looked* faint.

He wanted to get her out of there for a number of reasons, but he also knew he couldn't leave. Not until he'd finished one of the only things he was good at. Investigating.

"Okay," he said again, even though nothing really was okay at all. "Go wait in the living room. Don't—"

"—touch anything. I know." She still looked thoroughly shaken, and now resigned, as well. She turned sideways, her arms crossed and head ducked, giving the sheriff as wide a berth the narrow hallway would allow as she sidled past him.

"What've we got?" Dave plunked his evidence kit—an oversize toolbox—on the floor. "I didn't see any signs of forced entry."

As he reached for a pair of gloves from the kit, Holt could see Molly hovering in her living room. She still needed dry clothes. He blew out a breath and turned to the sheriff, telling him what they'd found.

Dave's eyebrows rose a little. "Sounds like she's as paranoid as Harriet Martel was," he muttered. "She probably forgot to lock her front door, and the rest is just reading too many whodunits."

Holt finished individually bagging each towel and handed them to the sheriff. "Harriet was paranoid?"

"She was always calling in complaints of strangers. People snooping around her house. No wonder, considering she lived the-hell-and-gone on the edge of town." Dave tossed the bags into the hall. "I suppose you're going to want to dust for fingerprints or some fool notion."

"Yeah, I'm a real idiot when it comes to collecting evidence," Holt said flatly. "But I guess someone had better be since you did the initial crime scene at Harriet's and managed to completely miss the book she'd written those initials on. If it hadn't been for Harriet's nephew, that damned book would still be sitting on the desk in Harriet's house sealed up behind a mile of crime-scene tape and we'd have even *fewer* leads to go on in a case where leads are nearly non-existent."

He stepped around the sheriff, who at least had the good sense to look a little ashamed, and went into the bedroom. He carefully collected the pillows from Molly's bed, as well as the little white bedspread thing.

Holt looked at the closet door. It was closed. Latched. He rubbed at the pain in his forehead. What kind of man would come in and rearrange pillows, towels and closets? In L.A. he'd seen nearly every twisted behavior imaginable. This was mild in comparison. Towels and pillows and clothes. Little, odd things that were enough to instill pure fear in a quiet, mysterious woman.

"And just what do you think you're gonna find on that stuff?" his boss asked when Holt carried everything out in bags to the hall and added to the ones already there.

"Proof of an intruder? An ex-husband with a motive for murder?" Holt turned back to the room, supremely irritated with his boss. Hell, *irritated* was too mild a word. He was annoyed. Pissed. He knew it was a long shot, but considering the lack of forward movement on the murder case, a long shot was better than nothing at all.

And Molly was still standing there in her living room, looking lost and rumpled and wet in her transparent dress. She'd pulled an afghan around her shoulders, at least.

Dave snorted. "You're on a wild-goose chase with that one, Deputy. This *intruder* story has got diddly to do with Harriet's case."

The sheriff could well be right, and Holt knew it, even if he didn't like it. "Well, unless you're telling me to ignore a citizen's complaint, I guess we'll see about that. And since we're talking about wild-goose chases, there were no complaints filed by Harriet for trespassers. Nothing of that nature at all." He knew. He'd gone over Harriet's case so many times he could recite the reports backward and forward. But if she had been afraid of intruders, maybe that was why the antigun woman had actually gotten herself one.

Dave was unperturbed. "Small towns," he reminded Holt, for all the world just a good-ol'-boy sheriff set on educating his not-too-bright citified deputy. "Not everything gets written up...when a friendly call by the authorities will calm down the situation with no harm done or no bags of so-called evidence being necessary."

Holt kept his eyes deliberately away from the sheets on Molly's bed. His fingers had brushed them, and they were about as fine and soft as...well, as soft as her skin was. "Considering her murder, I'd have thought such complaints by Harriet might have been relevant. And if Rumor is the place where crime is practically nonexistent, now we've got two women who happened to work at the library together, both complaining about trespassers. You gonna tell me that's a coincidence, too?"

Dave shook his head. He pulled out a pistachio and pried it apart. "You got a suspicious mind there, Holt. Waste your time if you want, then."

Holt took a thick terry robe off the hook on the back of Molly's door and strode past his boss, who'd begun looking a bit annoyed himself.

He went out to living room and handed the robe to Molly, then went to the bookcase.

"Oh. Do you...have to take the book?" Both hands clutched the robe tightly to her chest.

"Still reading it?"

"I'm always reading it."

He glanced at her, surprised at her wry tone. "Hard book to put down?"

"Hard concept to learn," she corrected wearily.

"Are you, um, done in the bathroom? I want to change."

"No, I'm not done. Was there anything else here that's been disturbed?"

"No."

"You haven't looked in the kitchen."

"I don't need to," she said evenly. "He never touched anything in the kitchen before." She slipped through the swinging door to the room in question and returned a moment later wearing the robe, her feet bare.

He immediately slammed down a barricade on thoughts of what lay beneath that pale-yellow terry cloth. "You're referring to your ex-husband. Thompson."

"Yes."

"Did Harriet help you the way she helped Darla Hostetler?"

Her chin lifted. "I don't know any Darla Hostetler. I told you that."

"Yeah, well, maybe we better not get into what you have or haven't told me," he said. He bagged the book.

"Oh, *now* you tell me to be quiet? You've been harassing me all this time to tell you the least little thing, but now—" Her mouth snapped shut and her eyes focused on the floor when the sheriff ambled into the room, his arms filled with evidence bags.

"Well, I guess I'll dump this off at the station, then get back to my evening supper. My Dee Dee, she cooked up a fine meal. Had to leave her alone with my old friend Henry Raines, and you know what a ladies' man he considers himself to be."

"I'm sorry for causing all this trouble." Molly's voice was hushed.

Dave was suddenly all smiles, as if he just then realized how thoroughly subdued Molly was. "Oh, now, don't you worry your little head none about that. You know," he said thoughtfully, "maybe you'd better just come on home with me while the deputy, there, finishes doing his thing."

Chapter Eight

Dave's invitation hung in the air, and right before Holt's eyes, Molly shrank into herself. "I couldn't possibly."

"Sure you could," the sheriff encouraged. "Give Dee Dee a chance to fuss over somebody besides our brood. You know my wife and how she just loves to fuss over anybody and everybody."

If he hadn't been watching Molly so closely, Holt would have missed the shudder that ran through her. "Thank you for the offer." Her words were stiff. "But I'll be fine here."

"You're sure, now?"

"She said so, didn't she?" Holt eyed Dave over Molly's downturned head, wishing the other man would just drop it.

"All right. But the offer's open anytime. You know us folks in Rumor. Friendly as the day is long.

Holt, I'll have somebody drop off your unit. I saw it was still parked over at the station when I drove by." Dave tossed another nut in his hand, and with a friendly smile, headed out the door.

Molly sank down on her couch as if all the energy had oozed out of her right along with the sheriff's departure. The sleeves of her yellow robe were too long and she'd tucked her hands up inside them. The length was long enough, too, that it completely covered her legs, leaving only the tip of her toes showing. Barely a sliver of skin showed beneath the tightly belted lapels, but it was enough to madden him.

He turned abruptly. *The job. Remember the job.* "I'm going to dust the bathroom for prints. The stuff is messy, but I'll do what I can to leave things clean."

"You won't find any prints." She popped off the couch and followed him down the hall.

His jaw tightened. He stopped in front of the bathroom once again. "Because there was no intruder in the first place?"

"Because he'll have wiped down everything with cleanser and a sponge."

She went into the bedroom and he heard a loud thump. Going after her, he saw that she'd opened the closet and was yanking clothes, hangers and all, from inside, pushing them into the hard-sided suitcase she'd opened across her white sheets.

"What the hell are you doing?"

"Gosh. Looks like packing. Feels like packing. Must...be...packing." Her voice was tight.

"You've disturbed the scene."

"Too bad." She pulled another armful of clothes

from the closet rod. "It doesn't matter, anyway. Rob never left any evidence. He knew the rules too well for that. And even if he had, it wouldn't have mattered, because he was too well protected."

"Protected? By what? You're sounding like a mafia ex-wife."

She jammed her armful onto the top of the colorful mound inside the case and slammed the lid. But it was too full. The latches wouldn't even reach each other. "No." She lifted the lid and yanked out two sweaters, then slammed shut the case and this time managed to fasten it. "But I might as well have been. It was just as bad. The brotherhood watching out for the brotherhood."

She dragged the suitcase off the bed, and it slammed against her legs, making her sway.

But he didn't dare reach for the thing, not when her eyes were glazed with emotion he understood just a little too well. Pain. Total and complete resignation to some awful fate.

He'd been at the end of his rope, not too long ago. And he still didn't like thinking about it. If his partner's wife hadn't left him the clipping with the notice for the opening with the Rumor Sheriff Department, he'd have probably found some way to end up in the same state as his partner.

Dead.

"Molly, you're in a robe and bare feet with a car sitting at the repair shop. Nothing can be as bad as you're afraid of. Where do you think you're going to go?"

Her soft lashes swept down. "What does it matter to you? I'm just a lying woman who's been standing in the way of your murder investigation."

"It matters, okay?" He raked his fingers through his hair. "Dammit, but you are one contrary female. If you are so intent on leaving this house, then why the hell not take up the sheriff on his offer? His house is enormous. He and Dee Dee would have room for you, at least. Hell, I'll drive you over there myself just as soon as my truck gets here."

"No!"

"Are you afraid the sheriff will find out who you really are?"

Her lips pressed together and he knew they weren't going to get anywhere. Not now.

She'd been so close to opening up, and now he felt as if they were no further ahead than they'd been the day she'd sat in front of his desk stoically answering questions about how she'd come to discover poor dead Harriet.

He shoved his hands in his pockets. She may have changed into a nice dry robe, but he was still in wet clothes. Just as well. Cold, uncomfortably damp denim helped keep his mind right where it belonged. On the job. "Then you can go to a motel, or go to a friend's, but no way in hell are you going to leave town."

Her lips worked before sound escaped. "You can't force me to stay."

"I could hold you for a day without officially charging you with anything. Or there's always the handy protective custody. I could lock you in a cell for that, honey. Given your insistence that someone broke in here tonight, and rifled through your unmentionable towels and frilly little pillows, I couldn't in good conscience leave you out there on your own to face God only knows what kind of threat." He hated the words, hated the fact that he felt like garbage for playing that particular card. But there really was no way that he was going to let her walk—run—away from Rumor. "It's painfully obvious that you don't want to stay here, Molly."

"So I should be satisfied with the alternative? You know I can't afford a motel, not when I've got to pay for the repairs to the car. As for friends—" Her mouth slammed shut again.

"You'd have plenty of friends if you stopped holding everyone at arm's length."

"Oh, that's rich, Deputy. Talk about the pot calling the kettle."

"This isn't about me. It's about you, and the fact that you don't want to stay under this roof."

Molly curled her hands into fists. Anger was futile, but at least it wasn't as debilitating as the panic that seemed to have flattened her earlier. "I don't like the choices."

Holt shrugged, as if he didn't care in the least. He merely rummaged in that box of stuff the sheriff had left and went into the bathroom. Through the doorways she watched him crouch down in front of the pedestal sink and tilt his head this way and that, looking at the pristine porcelain.

She shut her door far more forcibly than necessary and quickly pulled on jeans and a T-shirt. She shoved her feet into tennis shoes and scooped her hair back into a ponytail. Her purse was still in the living room. And though she thought she could make do without the driver's license—Harriet had helped her produce the identification necessary to obtain it—she needed the money in her purse, at the very least.

Only she didn't know how to safely get past Holt.

And if she did, *where* would she go?

Rob would surely be watching her, ready for the slightest move on her part. Undoubtedly feeling thoroughly satisfied that he'd been successful at smoking her out of hiding after all this time.

It's what he did for a living, after all. Smoking people out, as he used to put it.

She sank down on the end of the bed.

There was no way she could leave. No way she could stay.

And what if Holt was right? What if Rob *had* been involved in Harriet's murder? What if he'd somehow found out how Harriet had helped her change her name, provided her with a job, assisted her in making a new life for herself, and decided to extract his own twisted revenge on the innocent woman? Just because Molly had been the sole focus of Rob's lunacy in the past didn't mean that he couldn't have changed.

Had doing a thoroughly unselfish deed for an absolute stranger whom she'd met in the rest room at a librarian's conference led to the death of Harriet and her unborn child?

Molly shoved her fist against her mouth, holding back a moan.

Was it all her fault, then, after all?

Her bedroom door swung open and she looked mutely at Holt, not even able to summon indignation at his walking in without so much as a perfunctory knock. *You are most definitely* not *in control.*

"You were wrong," Holt said flatly. "There were prints all over the sink."

Her hand fell away from her mouth. "What?" She bounded off the bed. Relief warred with disbelief.

Relief that the intruder might not have been Rob. Disbelief that the man would have ever changed his ways. "But that's not what—"

"Your fingerprints." He held up two plastic-covered cards. "This is the one from the glass last Sunday." He shook the one on the right. "And this is from the sink." He jiggled the one on the left. "You didn't touch the sink when we came in. I was watching you the entire time, and you didn't even step foot into the bathroom. The prints weren't from tonight, the sink had not been wiped clean, and there were nobody else's prints but these that I'm pretty certain are yours."

She shook her head. "No, that can't be. Rob always wiped down the sink and the tub. Five times, Holt, five times I made a report, and five times the evidence technicians came out and found the same result. Five times! Why would he change his methods now?"

"Because he wasn't here at all? Maybe because nobody was here at all?"

Molly stared. "You still think I'm lying."

He set the fingerprint samples on the dresser just inside her doorway. "Molly, I don't know what to think. And right now, I'm too damned tired to get into it." He picked up the suitcase she'd left lying on the bed. "It's been a long day. Come on."

"I'm not going to let you lock me up in a jail cell!"

"And I'm not going to lock you in one, unless you give me no choice!" His voice rose.

So did hers. "Then where are you taking me?"

He raked back his hair again. She was surprised to see that as it dried a hint of wave had appeared in it. A wave that caused his hair to tumble across his forehead in a way that made her fingers itch to brush it back.

"I'll take you to Chelsea Kearns's place," he said, looking as irritated as she felt. "You ought to be safe enough there and she can make sure you don't run off in those little pink sneakers of yours."

"I can't go there! Her wedding is in a few days."

"It is?" Holt frowned a little then shrugged. "Okay, then we'll swing by Callie and Nick Sullivan's place."

"They're newlyweds." Molly's face went hot. "I'm not some unwanted pet for you to drop off at the most convenient place."

"Definitely not unwanted," he muttered. "Well, what do you suggest, middle-name Molly? Because unless I get you someplace where you're not gonna feel so panicked that you'll run off without a thought to your or anyone else's safety, I'm gonna strip off these damned wet jeans that are driving me up the wall right here and now. And I'm pretty sure you'd freak out at the notion of having a guy in his skivvies inside your sanctuary of a little home."

Her lips parted. How could she have forgotten that he'd gotten nearly as wet out in the park as she had? "What about your place?" The thought popped into her head and right out her mouth before she could think twice. Before she could even *think*. Otherwise, she'd have never said such a thoroughly unsuitable thing.

"Never mind," she said hurriedly. "If m-my fingerprints were on the sink, then maybe it *was* my imagination working overtime, and there's no reason for me not to stay here after all."

His jaw was cocked to one side, the edge of his teeth looking more white than ever against his ever-darkening bristled jaw. "Then I'll stay here with you."

"What?"

He turned away. "You heard me."

She nearly tripped over her feet as she dashed after him, only to find him crouched in the hallway, fitting tubes and brushes and little pots of powder back into the large toolbox. She stared at his broad back. The T-shirt he wore stretched tightly between his shoulder blades. He really did have a magnificent body. So tall and lean.

With shoulders wide enough to hold the problems of the world.

The thought appalled her. She didn't need a man to lean on. Nor one to shoulder her burdens in life. She was more than capable of taking care of herself. Hadn't she been proving that over and over again during the past eighteen months? "You can't stay here. I don't *want* you here. I don't want *anyone* here."

"Yeah. You've made that perfectly clear. Why is that, anyway?"

"Because—" She crossed her arms tightly. No. He wasn't going to find it that easy to pry into her mind. "It's none of your business."

He looked over his shoulder at her. "Honey, everything about you is my business as of tonight."

Her lips parted. For some reason, the statement didn't send her into a state of panic the way it should have. "Why? Because I admitted that Harriet mentioned a journal?"

"That. Among other things." He closed up the

box and stood with it in hand. The other hand, he held out to her. "Come with me."

She ignored the hand and the fingers that beckoned in demand. "No. What other things?"

His hand dropped, and he looked very much as if he were searching for some divine understanding when his head tilted back and he stared up at the ceiling. He let out a long breath and looked at her again. "Why is it that you're perfectly argumentative with me, but you practically cowered around the sheriff?"

"I don't like him!"

Now Holt looked amused. "And you like me? I'm touched."

"In the head, maybe." Despite her protest, Molly grabbed her purse and followed him out the door to his SUV after he locked her front door. Because there was no way she wanted to be left alone in the house, she assured herself. It didn't have *anything* to do with the deputy, personally.

The assurance felt weak. As weak as her knees were from thinking that Rob may have managed to find her, despite her excruciatingly careful efforts of the past year and a half.

Holt's truck was waiting at the curb just as the sheriff had promised, and Holt stuck the evidence kit in the back of the SUV before opening the passenger door for Molly.

The keys were already in the ignition. Proof of the way the people in this town were used to operating. On trust and the belief that nothing bad ever happened there.

It was one of the lures Harriet had used when she'd offered Molly a way out.

She slowly stepped up into the high vehicle where, sitting, she was on eye level with Holt. And she wondered when she'd gotten sort of used to the idea of actually being eye to eye with the man.

Maybe when he'd lain in the grass while the sprinklers sprayed over them, and she'd somehow taken comfort in his quiet, calm presence.

She deliberately untwisted her fingers and drew in a breath. Maybe Angel Ramirez was right and she should start participating in the groups at the shelter in Whitehorn, instead of just doing the literacy and reading groups every Monday evening. "The sheriff reminds me of my ex-husband." Excruciatingly so. She wanted to wretch whenever the man was near her.

Holt was silent for so long that she knew she'd surprised him with the admission.

"What, in looks?" he finally asked. "Dave's in his fifties."

"Rob's forty-two now. Fifteen years older than I am, and they do have similar qualities. That...that blond hair that's going gray at the temples. The sort of stocky build. A hearty smile for everyone...one that doesn't really reach their eyes. But that wasn't what I meant." She fell silent, nibbling at the inside of her cheek.

"All right." Holt's voice was soft. He stood inside the door and she could feel the warmth of him, smell the scent of wet grass from the park that still clung to him. "I'll bite," he said.

"Promise?"

His eyebrow peaked as dead silence fell between them.

Molly just wanted to crawl out the other door and

escape. She could not *believe* she'd said that. Goodness, she couldn't believe she'd even thought it!

"I mean, I want your p-promise that you won't do something with this information."

He leaned his shoulder against the door, seeming even broader and taller than before. "Since you haven't really given me much information from the start, I'm not real sure how to respond to that."

"How can you say that? I've told you about the journal now. And you know more about...about Rob than anybody except—"

"—except Harriet? Stop stalling, Molly. Why does the sheriff remind you of your ex?"

Molly swallowed. She'd been going to tell him, she reminded herself. She'd been going to explain it all. Until she'd walked up her porch steps and found her door unlocked and her sense of safety—minuscule though it was—disappeared in a puff.

"Molly?"

She cleared her throat. "Because Rob is a cop, too."

Holt closed his eyes, stifling an oath. He wasn't even shocked. But he should have figured it out. All the signs had been there. He needed to ask her more questions about Thompson, where he was assigned. What state, what city, precinct. So, of course, being the monumentally stupid man he was, he didn't. "I probably remind you of your ex-husband, as well."

He straightened away from the door, feeling more weary than he had since leaving California. But he went still when Molly touched his wrist. Her fingers were light. Cool. Yet the feel of them burned down in his gut, creating fires there was no possible way to quench.

Not with this woman. Not with what she'd endured.

She might be imagining the intruder in her house, she might be as paranoid as Dave suggested, or she might be completely right in believing that her ex-husband had somehow found her.

But Holt knew a woman who'd been pushed to her emotional limits when he saw one, and Molly's behavior so far was nearly textbook in that regard. Scumbag Rob Thompson had knocked her around, either emotionally or physically. In either case that meant it was hands-off for Holt.

Involvement with a hard case like him would only lead to more trouble, and nobody deserved that. Molly didn't need someone who only wanted— badly—to burn up some finely woven white sheets with her. She needed a man who possessed a wealth of tenderness and understanding and patience.

Definitely not him.

"Holt, I—"

He had to get her hands off him. "Never mind, Molly. I understand." He pushed her door closed and went around to the driver's side.

It was just as well, he told himself. He couldn't seem to manage to keep his head where it belonged when it came to one middle-name Molly Brewster. Knowing that every time she looked at him and saw the cop to whom she'd once been married ought to provide as effective a reminder as an icy cold wave on a windy morning.

No wonder she'd avoided the sheriff department unless she'd absolutely had no other choice. No wonder she'd nearly come unglued when he'd taken that fingerprint off her lemonade glass.

He reached for the ignition and started up the truck.

She might have all the cause in the world to hate men, to distrust cops.

But that still didn't mean Holt was prepared to trust her.

Chapter Nine

Holt's apartment, Molly discovered, held even fewer personal effects than hers did. She wouldn't have thought it possible, but as she stood in his living room waiting for him to do whatever it was he was doing back there, she realized it was, indeed, very possible.

He had a black leather couch that still smelled new. An old metal footlocker served as his coffee table, on which sat only a remote control. Undoubtedly for the big-screen television across the room. There were no magazines, no newspapers, no mementos on the shelf next to the television. Only a square piece of paper pinned to the wall with a thumbtack: a painting that looked as if it had been done in a child's hand. Green fields. Blue sky.

She wondered if the child who'd painted it was his. He'd never made any mention of family, a wife.

But then, he never made much mention of anything personal.

The galley-style kitchen opened right out into the living room, and he didn't even have a table. Only an unfinished wooden bar stool that sat beneath the narrow breakfast counter on the opposite side of the sink.

One bar stool.

It struck her as terribly lonely.

She stifled a yawn and finally perched on the edge of the couch. It was a lot more comfortable than the couch in her house, though, and as she continued to wait for the deputy, she finally slid back more fully, sinking into the soft leather.

A part of her wished he would hurry up and get his stuff together, because she wasn't all that comfortable sitting there in his almost-bare lonely living room. But the other part of her was no more comfortable with the notion that he'd be going back with her to *her* almost-bare lonely house for the night.

Her hand stroked across the butter-soft cushion beside her as another yawn escaped.

"It's been a long day."

She jumped, guiltily snatching back her hand, folding it in her lap. "I didn't hear you."

"Sorry." He didn't look it. He'd replaced his damp clothes with a fresh T-shirt and jeans. A zippered gym bag hung from a long canvas strap off his shoulder. "I forgot to ask you if you had a spare lightbulb."

"What?"

"So I can change the one on your porch."

She dragged her scrambled thoughts together, trying to think. "Um, I don't know."

He went into his kitchen, and she heard a cupboard open, then he came out, carrying a small carton containing a lightbulb. The same kind she'd chosen that day eight months ago when two strangers had bumped into each other in the hardware aisle. "Just in case," he said, and handed it to her to carry.

She smiled weakly. It was silly to think he'd remember the type of bulb she'd purchased that day. It was a common enough item, after all. He opened the door, waiting, and she hurried to her feet and followed him back out to his truck.

The small complex of apartments where he lived was located on the north side of Rumor. Almost out to the highway. And as they drove back through town, Molly swallowed, realizing how near to Harriet's house they'd been.

"It's a block farther out than my apartment," Holt's voice was quiet.

"What?"

"Harriet's house."

Molly frowned a little. Was he reading her mind?

"I think about her every time I drive to and from my place."

She shot him a look.

"I don't like murderers to get away with it."

She swallowed and looked down. There was room enough for an entire third person to sit on the bench seat between them, yet it still felt as if the interior of the vehicle was impossibly close. "But they do sometimes. People get away with all sorts of criminal behavior, never having to face any consequences at all."

"Not if I can help it." His voice was flat.

"How long have you been a—"

"Cop? Almost sixteen years. I went into the academy right after college."

"Young."

He made a soft sound. "Honey, I wasn't young even when I *was* young."

"Everybody should have a chance to be a child," she murmured, thinking of the fun she and Christina had had. Her sister was five years older than she was, but that hadn't kept them from being nearly inseparable.

"You won't get an argument from me."

He pulled up in front of the sheriff's station, but left the engine running. "Stay here."

"Aren't you afraid I'll steal your vehicle and skip town?"

Holt gave Molly a long look. He didn't doubt for a second that she wanted to skip and run. She still had a blanket of panic surrounding her that was nearly visible. "Aren't you afraid I'll leave you to your own devices to fight against your ex-husband, if in fact he's the one who broke into your house tonight?"

He watched a shudder ripple through her.

"That's what I thought. I won't be long." He turned and strode up to the door, unlocking it. He left a message for Sue of some things he wanted her to take care of in the morning, then went past the two jail cells, into the very back room.

He eyed the gun safe for a long moment.

He hadn't carried a piece since he'd come to Rumor. Not since he'd sat on a hard cement sidewalk on a perfect California night and held his bleeding partner in his arms.

He scrubbed his hands down his face. If Benny

were alive, he'd be laughing his ugly gray-bearded head right off and telling Holt to stop being a pansy.

Holt swore and undid the heavy combination lock, swinging open the thick metal door. There wasn't much inside. It wasn't as if the Rumor law enforcement had a need to house artillery. But Holt's weapon was there. On the same shelf where he'd stuck it eight months ago—the day he'd pinned on a badge for the Rumor Sheriff Department.

He pulled it out, ignoring how familiar the weight felt, and tucked it in the small bag he'd grabbed from his desk. He added his holster, ammunition and a cleaning kit, then zipped up the bag and relocked the safe.

Without a backward glance, he locked up the office again and climbed into the truck beside Molly, who hadn't budged so much as an inch.

A few minutes later they were at her house.

"I'll go in first."

"No." She shook her head and opened her door. "I'm not a coward."

He caught her arm, feeling the way her muscles tensed. "Nobody said you were, Molly."

"Then why am I afraid to sleep by myself under my own roof?"

"Experience."

She frowned a little, and when she tugged at her arm, he let her go. "Rob wouldn't have left without wiping down the sink."

"Are you trying to convince me or yourself?"

She hopped down out of the vehicle. "Maybe us both," he heard her say.

Moving fast, he caught up with her before she could unlock the front door. They'd been gone less then thirty minutes, but it didn't take even a tenth of that for a determined person to get into a locked house. He nudged Molly to the side of the dark doorway and took the keys from her hand. "Humor me. Wait."

She silently padded back down the porch steps and crossed her arms. "Okay. I'm waiting."

He unlocked the door and quickly, thoroughly, checked the house, then went back outside. "You can go in now," he told her as he headed back to his truck to grab his gear.

She hadn't moved when he headed back up to the house. Her eyes searched his. "You really do believe me that someone was in my house tonight."

He blew out an impatient breath. "Don't go disillusioning me with lies *now,* Molly."

"I didn't lie."

"Okay, then. Let's just…get through the night, then, shall we?"

"And in the morning?"

Now who was lying? He'd already put some things into motion, namely finding out if there was a cop named Rob Thompson in any of the nearby states. "We'll figure that out when morning comes," he said.

After a moment she turned and led the way back inside her house. He dumped his two bags on the floor by the couch, then took the fresh lightbulb she was still carrying from her. "I'll change the other one for you."

"I'll, um, m-make up the couch for you. I'm afraid it's not terribly comfortable."

"It'll do."

During the course of his career, he'd slept in cars,

alleys and on rooftops. A too-short, flowered couch would not kill him. Knowing that he was under the same roof as the woman who turned him on simply by drinking a malt, however, just might.

Feeling thoroughly annoyed all over again, Holt went out to the porch and thumbed loose the fastenings for the simple opaque globe that covered the lightbulb. Sliding the globe away, he touched the bulb, ready to unscrew it, but as soon as he did, it gave out a little burst of light.

He went still.

The bulb wasn't burned out.

It had been unscrewed. Just enough to keep it from working, but not so much that it would fall out of the socket.

Frowning, he finished twisting the bulb until it was snug, then replaced the globe and went back inside.

Molly was flipping a pale-yellow blanket over the couch that she'd already covered with a white sheet. "Bulb was just loose."

She whirled around, the blanket dropping from her fingers. "Oh. Well, I should have thought of that. It does that sometimes." She picked up the blanket and started smoothing again.

"You said that you'd made five reports on your ex-husband. All for the same thing?"

Again the blanket fell. "Um, yes."

"Was he charged?"

"With what? Nobody ever believed that he'd broken into my home. They just thought it was one more complaint by the crazy woman with a vindictive imagination."

"How long were you married to him?"

Her throat worked. He wasn't sure she'd answer

him. Not even after the scare she'd had. "Two years." She smoothed her hand over her ponytail. Toyed with the tiny gold hoop in her ear. "He, um, he was very angry when I moved out and filed for divorce."

"He hit you?"

Her mouth clamped shut.

"Molly, I can't help you if you won't help me a little. I know you don't want to trust me, but not every police officer is like your ex-husband."

She headed for the hallway, and he blew out a long sigh.

"Once." Her voice floated back down the hallway. "He only hit me once. And I left him for it."

Then he heard the sound of her bedroom door shutting.

He ran his hand around the back of his neck and looked down at the couch that had been made into a sort of bed.

Well, Tanner. You wanted to know what it'd be like to sleep on her soft sheets. Now you'll know.

"Your couch has a broken spring in it."

Molly bobbled her coffee cup and barely managed to set it on the kitchen table without spilling the contents over herself. She looked up at Holt and just as quickly looked away. It didn't seem to matter, though.

His image was seared into her brain.

It was unimaginable that he'd slept on her couch the previous night. Even more unimaginable that *she'd* actually been able to sleep in her own bed, knowing he was under her roof, particularly after thinking that Rob might have found her.

But sleep she had.

Soundly.

Dreamlessly.

For the first time since she'd discovered Harriet's body, she'd slept through the night without one nightmare disturbing her.

"I know it does. I warned you that you wouldn't be comfortable on it. The bathroom's yours. I'm finished there." She made herself offer the words. It was only polite. But she started thinking about him standing in the tub surrounded by the clear shower curtain that hung from old-fashioned porcelain and chrome rings, wearing nothing but water and soapsuds.

She hurriedly spooned sugar into her coffee, even though she'd already sweetened it before he'd come into the kitchen wearing nothing but a pair of gray sweatpants that hung dangerously low over his lean hips.

No man had a right to look that good at seven in the morning after spending the night on a flowered couch with a sprung spring.

"Is there more coffee?" His voice sounded rusty, and his eyes were barely open as he aimed for the counter.

"Pot's right in front of you, Deputy. I'm thinking that you're not much of a morning person." Feeling immeasurably more cheerful all of a sudden, she forced down a sip of the coffee, barely managing not to gag on the too-sweet stuff.

He cast her a sidelong glance. "Depends on who is next to me when I wake up."

Her cheeks went straight from warm to broil. No stop, no waiting. She quickly shoved her newspaper and several books into her soft-sided briefcase and stood. "Well, I'm off."

"An hour early?" He'd poured his coffee and turned around to lean back against the counter as he drank it straight down, seeming unperturbed by the fact that it was steaming hot. "What's the rush?"

"I...need to start moving my things into Harriet's office."

His dark brows rose a little. "Again. What's the rush?"

She had no answer. Nothing that would make any sense, at any rate. The excuse had been just the first thing to pop into her head. She'd been avoiding dealing with Harriet's office for two weeks, already. "There are eggs in the fridge," she said instead. "You might as well help yourself."

"Gracious as ever," he murmured, and poured a little more coffee into his cup. "Before you race out of here like the devil is after you, I'm coming with you to the library this morning, by the way—"

"You are not."

"I was wondering about the picture on your bookcase. And yes. I am."

She pressed her fingertips to her temple. "Why?"

"Do we need to repeat the whole song and dance again?" He'd braced one hand against the counter beside him, and the muscles in his arm stood out distinctively. "I'm game if you are, but I'd have thought you would pretty much have it memorized by now."

"Why were you wondering about the photograph?"

"It's the only one in the place. Seems to be the only one, anyway."

"It is." She left the kitchen, not really wanting to think about all the personal effects she'd had to leave behind when she'd walked away from her home in Wyoming. She'd kept only one small photograph of Christina tucked away in her wallet, and that was it.

"So? What's the deal with it?"

She should have known he wouldn't leave the matter alone. "It's just a photograph. From one of my reading groups. The first one I started when I came to Rumor."

"Harriet's in the picture. You said she wasn't involved in any of the reading groups."

"She wasn't." Molly picked up the small, framed photo and studied it. "But the week before she died, she approached me and asked if we'd like to have the meeting out at her home."

"Did she say why?"

"No." She gently slid her thumb across the glass. "She seemed happier than usual. I don't know. Softer. Maybe it was because she knew she was pregnant, even though she hadn't shared that news with anybody that I know of. Maybe it's all just my imagination."

"Probably not. Harriet was forty-three years old and childless. A pregnancy might have been her life's dream."

Molly nodded faintly. She really and truly wished that Holt would put on a shirt. Not that she had anything particularly against the view of his chest, with the smattering of dark hair that stretched across the miles of hard muscle, but it was particularly… distracting. And she would choke before she'd admit it to him. He would undoubtedly figure a way to turn the knowledge to his advantage.

"Well, in any case," she said, clearing her throat, "this particular group met at her house the, um, the Thursday before she…died. One of the women had one of those cameras, you know. The disposable kind. She snapped off this shot of us there in front of Harriet's fireplace. We had to push two armchairs out of the way to make room for—"

"The chairs. Were there pillows on them?"

Molly frowned. "I don't know. I didn't notice. Yes, maybe."

"Maybe."

"I don't remember! Everything in Harriet's house was precise and orderly. So, yes, she probably did have pillows on the chairs. I know the chairs matched. I remember them from when I went there when I came to town. We sat in the chairs and discussed the job."

"But you don't remember if there were matching pillows."

She pressed her fingertips to her temples. "Holt, I…" She sighed, shaking her head. "I just don't know. Why does it matter? She wasn't suffocated with a pillow, she was shot by a gun."

"Through, we're fairly certain, one of the pillows," Holt said evenly. "There was only one pillow present at the scene. The other is missing."

"Oh." Molly grimaced. "Be nice if you could find the pillow sitting in someone's garage or something, wouldn't it."

"Yeah. Nice. Unlikely. So, tell me more about that night."

She thought. "Well, I remember being surprised about all the candles. She'd put candles inside the fireplace, as well as on the mantel, and they were all lit. Harriet never seemed the sort for that kind of romantic touch. But then, I was also surprised at the book she'd chosen to discuss with the reading group. *Les Liaisons Dangereuses. Dangerous Liaisons.*''

He went still beside her. ''Romance and revenge.''

''Yes. And lots of it. Betrayal, too. It's French, you know. From the late 1700s.''

''All I know about the story, I learned from the movie.''

She glanced up to see him staring into his coffee mug. ''Anyway, that was the book Harriet wanted to discuss. Which worked fine. The whole group had already read it before—it's a romance group, you see—and so it was a simple matter of everyone skimming through it to refresh themselves with the story.''

''And you didn't think it odd that Harriet, out of the clear blue sky, suddenly decided to get chummy with you and your reading group.''

''Well, no.'' Molly sighed a little. ''Maybe loneliness was beginning to wear on her or something. There was never any question that she wouldn't be welcomed to any one of the groups, though frankly I'd have thought she'd lean more toward the mystery genre than romance. But that wasn't the group who was meeting that week. Romance was.''

''Are all the members of this particular group in the photograph?''

Molly counted the women in the photo, thinking back to that night. ''No, actually. Dee Dee Reingard was supposed to be there, but her littlest one had come down with an ear infection, so she'd called and canceled. And Helen Packer isn't in the photo, because she was the one behind the camera taking the picture.''

''Did everyone have their own copy of the book?''

''Pretty much. Dee Dee sent hers along for Miriam Hughes to use, because Miriam's book collection was destroyed last year in the fire they had. Such a shame. She had quite an extensive collection, I heard.''

''And Harriet? She had her own copy.''

''Yes. Heavens, you must have seen Harriet's bookshelves. These ones in the photo that flanked the fireplace were just a small sampling of what she had built in her bedroom. Some of the volumes she had were first editions, very rare. Worth a fortune.'' She looked up at Holt. ''I don't know why I didn't think of that before!'' She unthinkingly grabbed his forearms, her fingers curling against the hard strength. ''Is that a motive, Holt? Robbery? Maybe Harriet was never meant to have been harmed at all!''

Chapter Ten

Molly waited, her heart charging in her chest. If it were a robbery involving rare books, there might be a way to trace it. Collectors dealt in rare books, and collectors usually kept scrupulous records. "Holt? What do you think? Were any of the books taken from Harriet's room?"

He shook his head. "It's a good idea, Molly. But every book was accounted for. Harriet had a listing of them all in her desk. She seemed pretty organized that way."

"Oh." Thoroughly deflated, she realized she was still clutching his arm and quickly let go.

"Helen Packer," he said. "Tell me about her. And the Hughes woman."

"Miriam?"

"Yeah."

Molly rubbed her earring. "Well, Helen is sort of

new to town. She and her husband moved here right around the same time you did, as I recall. Pretty quiet, eclectic tastes in books. She's the newest member of the group. Miriam's one of the original members. That's her,'' she pointed to the tall, spare-looking woman standing behind Harriet. ''You've surely met her around town. In her fifties, I'd guess. Lives somewhere down south of Cave Springs Road. Pretty far out from town, I think, otherwise they might have saved more when she and her husband had that fire. Why?''

He frowned again, still staring into his coffee as if he were trying to read something. ''Harriet tried to write something,'' he said finally. ''On the back of her book, that *Dangerous Liaisons*. Initials.''

Molly closed her eyes, far too vividly recalling the scene she'd found at Harriet's a month earlier. The book had been sitting on the desk right in front of poor Harriet. ''The book was faceup.''

''Yeah.''

''You said she wrote on the back of it.''

''Right. Probably how the blood got smudged. She turned it over. Her killer turned it over. Somebody moved it.''

''Blood?''

''The initials were written in her own blood.''

Molly focused hard on the photograph until the burning behind her eyes subsided. ''So, the initials...obviously not enough to identify someone for certain, or you'd have arrested somebody by now.''

He nodded briefly.

''Well, maybe it wasn't initials,'' she suggested hesitantly. ''Maybe she was trying to write a word. What were the letters?''

He looked at her. "I shouldn't have even told you there *were* letters."

"Oh." She knew how investigations went. Still, it stung. "Of course." She started to put the photo back on the shelf, but Holt took it from her first. The brush of his fingers left hers tingling, and she curled them at her side, surreptitiously rubbing them against her pale-gray slacks.

"I've had my vaccine for cooties."

Her hand froze. She looked at him, mortified, but the slow glance he gave her in return was so unexpectedly rich with amusement, she just felt that unaccountable breathlessness all over again.

If the man ever laughed in her hearing, she feared she'd just pass out right then and there. Even if he *was* a cop.

"I've got to go."

"No, you don't. The library opens at eight. You can wait for me."

"But—"

"Molly, have you forgotten what happened here last night?"

"Of course not!"

"You wanna tell me where we can find Rob Thompson? To see if he's where he's supposed to be and not lurking around Rumor somewhere?" He waited a beat. "I didn't think so. Then, you know there's no way I'm going to let you go around unguarded. At least until we get the results back on your towels and pillows."

"Well, the results won't show anything," she said flatly.

"You so sure about that? You were wrong about the sink being wiped clean, after all."

She pressed her lips together, wishing there was a good argument, knowing that there wasn't. Also knowing that for the first time in forever, she didn't quite feel an inescapable need to *RUN!* at the notion that Rob might somehow be privy to her whereabouts.

"Wait for me."

She sighed and nodded, watching Holt through her lashes as he strode down the hallway, wearing only those nearly disgraceful gray sweatpants.

There was a spot on the back of his bare shoulder that looked a little sore, and she guiltily remembered the way the hood of her car had banged down on him. She hadn't even mended his shirt yet. She'd spot cleaned the bloodstain on it the previous night, but touching the fabric that enticingly smelled of him had been more than she could take, and she'd left the shirt still sitting in her tiny laundry room.

Out of sight, out of mind.

Right.

When she heard the bathroom door close, she sank onto the couch. Onto the right end, where the broken spring didn't affect the seating.

"Be honest, Molly," she whispered. "The only reason you don't feel a need to run from Rob right now is because Deputy tough-guy is with you."

She sighed shakily and sat back to wait. She was just fooling herself if she thought that Holt would turn out to be any different from the police in Wyoming when it came to protecting her from her ex-husband. No matter what he claimed, if he ever found out just *who* Rob was, he'd be like all the rest.

Holt didn't take all that long to get ready, and when he came out wearing a fresh uniform shirt tucked into faded jeans, a pair of scuffed, once-white athletic shoes on his feet, she felt as if she was nearly in control of her faculties again. It helped a lot that he barely looked like a cop, much less a small-town deputy sheriff.

Until she watched him adjust the holster at the small of his back and clip the gold badge to the front of his belt. "Mind if I take this picture and have it enlarged?"

"Of course not. Whatever helps."

His gaze drifted over her thoughtfully as he reached for the door. "Thanks."

She followed him outside, swallowing her indignation when he took her keys, and locked the door himself before handing them back to her. She shoved them into the side pocket of her briefcase and followed him out to the white SUV with Rumor Sheriff Department emblazoned in black on the side. "When did you start carrying a gun?"

He opened the door for her and held her briefcase while she climbed up inside. "Again," he said. "I started carrying a weapon again as of yesterday."

"Why again?" she asked, the second he'd rounded the vehicle and climbed behind the wheel. "The sheriff doesn't even carry a gun, that I've ever noticed. And he wears tan trousers, not jeans."

"You're kidding me, right?"

"No. I'm pretty sure the sheriff wears the entire uniform, not just the shirt."

He cast her a long look. "You're getting very sassy all of a sudden."

She almost laughed. She might have, if she didn't know now that he'd begun wearing his gun because of what had happened at her house. "Well, you don't seem to follow the sheriff's lead when it comes to things like that. I also overheard him giving you a hard time for taking my towels and pillows in for analysis.''

"Dave doesn't like admitting anything unsavory can happen under his nose. He's probably killing himself with guilt, too, over dismissing Harriet's complaints of trespassers as paranoia.''

"Paranoia?'' Molly echoed. "What on earth are you talking about?''

His glance was quick. "She never told you about trespassers around her house?''

"No.'' Her brows knitted. "But I...guess I'm not surprised. She didn't share personal matters like that with me. Only, I really wouldn't ever describe Harriet as the type to be paranoid.'' She looked away from his gaze that was much too intense. "That's more *my* speed,'' she added in a low voice.

"So you think if Harriet claimed that there was somebody casing her place or something to that effect, it was probably true.''

"I don't think she'd indulge in an overactive imagination. Now, are we going to sit here all morning, or are you going to get me to work on time? Because I could easily walk across the park—''

"Not on my watch.'' He drove down the street, slowing as a trio of kids darted across, heading toward the park.

The oversize towels tossed across their shoulders flapped behind them like colorful flags as they ran. And when one dropped the beach ball she was carrying, they all stopped and waited. Then with a thoroughly engaging grin and wave at Molly and Holt in the truck, the kids dashed off again.

"We're you ever that carefree?"

"Sure." Molly glanced at him. It was the second time he'd made some reference to being young. She was getting used to his solemn expression now, seeing that there were dozens of subtle shades to it. And as far as she could tell right now, he looked...sad.

"When I was little," she went on. "My sister and I loved summertime. We'd be at the town pool ready to swim even when the water was still cold enough that it left ice crystals on our skin when we dove in."

"Where'd you grow up?"

She very nearly answered him. Closing her mouth, she turned and looked out the side window. He might look sad at the thought of lost childhoods, but she wasn't going to fall for his tactics quite that easily.

"One of these days you're gonna have to trust me, Molly. Whether or not I wear a badge."

"Really. Like you trust me?" She raised her eyebrows and looked at him. "I notice you haven't returned that fingerprint from the glass to me. And that you had it handily nearby to match up against the prints you lifted from my sink. What were you doing with it? Carrying it around in your hip pocket?"

"My shirt pocket," he answered easily enough.

Molly's lips tightened. "All right, then. If we're going to talk about trusting each other, where did *you* grow up?"

He turned the corner, rounding the back side of the park. "Most people would say Los Angeles."

"What would *you* say?"

"My grandfather's farm."

"The one near Billings. Is he still alive?"

"No."

"Do you miss him?"

"He was ornery, pigheaded and stubborn. Yeah. I miss him."

Molly chewed the inside of her cheek, looking away, and they finished the short drive to the library in silence.

He waited while she unlocked the main entrance, and then followed her around as she turned on overhead lights and booted up the computer terminals. He followed her around long enough to make her more than a little nuts, until she finally bypassed all the little tasks she ordinarily did in the morning to prepare for the day and went into Harriet's office.

"Where do you want to start?"

She could feel the warmth of his body where he stood behind her, and took an instinctive step away. Then, feeling foolish because of it, she continued forward to one of the stacks of boxes against the wall. "I need to go through all the books in these boxes and decide whether to add them to our collection or send them somewhere else."

He'd joined her and reached in the top box, lifting a dusty hardcover from the pile. "Somewhere else? Like a garbage Dumpster?"

She took the book from him. "Oh, hush. There is almost always a home for books somewhere. Harriet was planning on going through these boxes before she…well, she never got to it. And I haven't had the time."

"Or the heart?"

Molly shrugged a little. "I suppose." She started to lift the box off the top of the pile, and with an impatient sound Holt lifted her hands away from the box and lifted it himself.

"Where do you want it?"

She focused fiercely on the desk, telling her heart to just settle right back down, as she quickly scooped up a stack of old yearbooks from the high school and plopped them on the floor beside the desk. "You can put the box there on the credenza. Thanks."

He put the box where she indicated and dusted off his hands. "Considering the inch of dust covering this, I doubt Harriet kept her journal in these boxes."

"Well, I don't know where else she might have put it. Unless it's at her home."

"It's not."

"And you've already checked her desk, right?"

"Yeah." His gaze ran over the large, aging piece of furniture. "Looks like Harriet believed in using a thing until its last gasp of life."

Molly tsked. "It's an antique desk, Holt. It's probably worth a small fortune or it would be if this sidepiece was removed and the original desk was restored."

"I s'pose it might be valuable to someone with a taste for old, ugly furniture," he agreed. "This thing would be in perfect company with Horton Jupe's fringed umbrella."

"Well, maybe I'll call Mr. Jupe and see if he's interested in taking it off our hands. I need my computer, and this desk won't work with one at all. The size is completely wrong."

"What about the desk you've already got?"

"The new assistant librarian will use it, I suppose. Or a suitable new one if I get rid of this one."

"Has somebody already been hired?"

Molly nodded, her mind more on the books that she was taking out of the box. She made two piles.

Discard and keep. "She starts in two weeks. She's moving here from Whitehorn. Vanessa McInnis. Here, would you mind putting these on the floor over there?" She waved her hand over the discard pile.

"Vanessa was my ex-wife's name." He moved the books and picked up the second box, setting it by her chair so she could reach it, too.

But Molly was staring at him, the books in her hands all but forgotten. "You were married?"

"I'm thirty-seven years old, you think there was no time to fit in a wife somewhere along the way?"

"How long?"

"Long enough, considering we ended up divorced." His voice was bland, not betraying one way or the other how he felt about the divorce. "Is there something special about those books you're still holding?"

"Oh. No." She stuck them in the keep pile and blindly reached into the box again, only to yank it back with a cry when her fingertip encountered something sharp.

Holt grabbed her hand before she could stick her finger in her mouth. "What is it?"

She stood, as much shocked by his gentle grip as she was by whatever had cut her fingertip badly enough to make blood well and overflow. "Something cut me." They both leaned over to look in the box, and Molly winced when their heads collided.

"Sorry," he muttered. He cupped his palm over her forehead where they'd bumped, still holding her other hand, and looked in the box. "There's broken glass in there," he said. "Nothing life threatening." He looked back at her. "We just need to get your finger cleaned and taped up."

His face was so close she could see each individual lash surrounding his coffee-brown eyes. Crows feet arrowed out in a faint web, more indicative of squinting in sunlight than constant smiles. And he had a scar, a small, thin white line, just below his left eyebrow.

"What happened there?" She unthinkingly lifted her free hand and brushed her fingertip over the scar.

He jerked back as if she'd jabbed him with a cattle prod.

Embarrassed beyond words, she straightened away, too, tugging her injured finger out of his grasp and grabbing a tissue from the box on the corner of Harriet's desk to hastily wrap around it. "I'm sorry." One tissue wasn't enough to stanch the blood, and she reached for more. "I don't know what I was thinking."

"I caught a broken bottle in a bar fight."

"Oh. Right." She smiled cheerfully. Anything to cover up the way she felt inside. Hot and cold and shivering, all at once. "You could have lost an eye that way," she chattered, reaching for another tissue to bunch around the others. Her finger really did seem to be bleeding quite a bit. And it had begun throbbing unmercifully. "I hope you succeeded in arresting him."

"Her. It was Vanessa who slashed me."

Her mouth dropped open, her nervous chatter suddenly ceasing. He pulled out a white cloth handkerchief from his back pocket and replaced the mess of tissues with it. His touch was so gentle, it made her eyes burn.

"I think you might actually need a couple stitches

after all,'' he said. ''But the pain of getting stitches can't be any worse than the pain you have now.''

''Your ex-wife hit you with a broken—''

''Beer bottle. She was still my wife at the time. But, yeah. She was a little pissed at me for decking her lover. Come on, I'll drive you. Right now. It's deeper than I thought.''

Somehow he'd managed to maneuver her around the desk and toward the door, even grabbing her purse along the way. Her mind was scrambling. His wife had cheated on him? ''But the library—''

''Will still be standing when we get back. And I know how you love to argue, but cooperate just this—''

''Only with you.''

''What?''

''I only argue with you.'' The realization was enough to make her tremble, and she dropped the keys he'd handed her. She *did* argue with him. And instead of towering over her, yelling angrily until she wanted to cower, he just kept right on talking, discussing, debating. And even when his voice did go up—and there'd been a few times it had gone up a lot—she still stood her ground.

With him.

He picked up the keys and locked the door himself after they exited. ''Lucky me,'' he said dryly. Then he smiled a little. And the fine web of lines extending from his eyes did crinkle up, after all.

Molly headed down the steps with him. He kept hold of her elbow, as if he feared she'd pass out from losing a few drops of blood, then carefully helped her into his truck. *No,* she thought, thoroughly bemused. *Lucky me.*

Chapter Eleven

"I thought tetanus shots were only necessary if you punctured yourself with rusty metal."

"Shows what you know." Holt stepped back into the curtained examining room of the hospital. "But now you're safe against rusty nails, too."

"Well, the shot hurt more than the cut," she said, sitting gingerly on the paper-covered table. A nurse had given her the injection, but she still was waiting for someone to stitch her finger. It had already been probed and prodded, even X-rayed, to ensure that there was no glass still buried deep inside it.

His lips tilted as he sat down on the little metal rolling stool. "Poor baby. I'd offer to kiss it better but figure you'd probably slap me."

She stared hard at the counter behind him. It was crowded with stainless steel canisters and stacks of tissue boxes. She scrambled for something to say.

Anything to say. Nothing came to mind, and she just sat there like a ninny, her cheeks hot. "I, um, wonder what's in the canisters."

He looked over his shoulder, and with a lazy push of his leg, rolled toward the counter. "Want me to look?"

"No! We're not supposed to look in there. That's just for the doctors and nurses."

One corner of his lips tilted. "Molly Brewster, you're a rule follower, after all."

She didn't have a chance to respond to that—not that she was sure how she would, anyway—because the curtain rattled again, and a boy in a white coat entered with a covered tray. "Okay, now, let's take a look at that finger," he said cheerfully.

Molly grimaced, staring at the boy's name tag. Figures. Doctor. Then she caught Holt's amused gaze over the lad's head and knew he was thinking the exact same thing.

A few minutes later the job was done, and the boy left. Probably to finish fourth grade.

Molly held up her hand for Holt's inspection. "Well. I think he has a thing for gauze." Her finger was covered in enough of the white stuff to make it look as if she'd cut open an artery rather than merely the tip of her middle finger.

He wrapped his fingers around her wrist, turning her hand this way and that. Then he ducked his jet-black head, and she went still as he pressed his lips to the thickly wrapped finger. "There. Now we can go."

As if nothing unusual had occurred, he gathered up her purse and the papers the doctor had left, and tugged back the curtain. "Unless you want to take up residence here for some reason,'' he added when she just sat there on the table.

She scrambled down and followed him out through the waiting room. He'd left his truck parked in a no parking zone. Holt *wasn't* so much of a rule follower.

He opened the passenger door, and she instinctively pressed her hands on his shoulders when he lifted her at the waist and set her inside. She looked at his mouth. Realized what she was doing and hurriedly swiveled on the seat, looking forward. "I've never had stitches before. Not ever."

"Yeah, you mentioned that a few times on the drive up here."

She couldn't tell if he was laughing at her or not as he went around to the driver's side. She jiggled her bandaged hand. It didn't hurt at all. Probably because of the enormous shot she'd been given that numbed it practically to the elbow. "Christina never had stitches, either, and she was always into one adventure or another. She broke her arm once, but never had to have stitches."

He looked over his shoulder to see if the way was clear, then began driving out of the emergency zone. "Christina."

"My, um, my sister."

"Hmm. Well, six stitches hardly even qualify as stitches."

"Oh, really. I suppose *you've* had dozens."

"Sixty-seven once."

She swallowed, suddenly feeling a little green. "Good...heavens. Not from the, uh, the beer bottle incident, I hope."

"Nah. That was minor in comparison."

"What happened?"

"A coked-up fourteen-year-old with a machete."

"Fourteen!"

"Gang members come in all shapes and sizes. Do you want me to drive you back to the library, or home?"

"The library, of course." Her voice was faint. "A little cut on my finger is certainly no reason to close the library down for the day. Harriet never closed the library before it was supposed to, you know. What happened to the, uh, the—"

"Knife wielder? We got him into rehab and he now helps run a community center in East L.A. He's twenty-four now."

"We."

"My partner. Benny. And me. We."

If Rob had ever been attacked by a gang member, he'd have choked before trying to actually *help* the boy.

Molly looked out the window as Holt left Whitehorn behind. It wouldn't take long to get back to Rumor. Not at the rate he was traveling. "How long were you and Benny partners?"

"Fourteen years."

A long time, she thought. "He must have missed you when you left to come here."

"No."

She glanced at him.

"He's dead."

Her lips parted. "Oh, Holt. I'm sorry. What happened?"

The question wasn't unexpected, but still Holt didn't answer. Not right away.

"Never mind. It's your business. I shouldn't have asked."

Holt blew out a sigh and automatically changed lanes to pass a slow-moving tractor that was cutting down the dried grass growing along the highway. He wanted Molly to trust him, to open up enough for him to get the information he needed.

If Sue had read the message he'd left for her the night before, then she was already discreetly checking for Rob Thompsons. He knew she'd sent the pillows and towels from Molly's place on to a lab in Whitehorn first thing that morning, because he'd called the lab while Molly was having her finger X-rayed.

They hadn't gotten to them yet—probably wouldn't for a few days yet, and no amount of persuasion or begging had convinced them to move the stuff up in priority. He'd even called Chelsea Kearns to see if she could throw some weight around, and she'd had no luck, either.

The only thing Chelsea had done was remind him of her wedding on Saturday. "I want my friends there," she'd said. "So be sure to make the time to be there. Bring a guest, too, if you want."

Time. He didn't want to take out time for a wedding, but he supposed it didn't matter in the end. Everything about the case was taking too damned much time.

He could find out what Molly was hiding, given time. But he wanted her to trust him. He just wasn't sure when he had reached the point where he wanted her trust for reasons other than making his investigation a helluva lot easier.

The highway stretched out straight and true before

them, cutting through the fields on either side like a ribbon of black. Overhead, fat white clouds drifted in the sky that was so blue it looked as if it had been painted with a kid's watercolor paintbrush. Like the painting hanging in his apartment. Benny's grandson had given it to Holt at the birthday celebration Benny and Joy had insisted on throwing for him.

"My partner died in a shooting at a convenience store," he said abruptly. Leaving behind Joy and Benny Jr., the grandson they'd been raising as their own.

"Holt, really, you don't have to—"

"We were off duty. And it was a setup."

"Holt—"

"Because we'd helped take down five officers in the department who'd been in collusion with a particular gang."

He looked at Molly, letting his words sink in. Watching her eyes widen just a bit, her long, pretty throat—right above the buttoned-up pointy collar of her pink blouse—work.

"Just because they were cops," he added, just in case she needed elaboration, "didn't mean they could get away with being criminals."

And just because he and Benny had nailed the dirty cops, didn't mean the story ended there.

Swallowing the pain that he wasn't sure would ever go away, he looked over at Molly. She didn't say a word, just looked at him with those wide aquamarine eyes of hers for a long, long while.

Long enough for him to feel sweat on his spine despite the truck's powerful air conditioner, which blasted over him.

Long enough for him to almost forget who he was

and what he was and why he was driving down a highway with the town's librarian beside him.

"I'm sorry about your partner," she finally said.

Then she turned and looked out the window, resting her head against the high back seat.

Holt's fingers curled over the steering wheel.

So much for sharing life stories.

"Deputy, there is a call for you."

Both Holt and Molly looked up when the volunteer—Mrs. English—appeared in the doorway. They were sitting in Harriet's office, surrounded by piles of books. On the floor. On the desk. On the narrow ledge of the window.

Books, books, books. Everywhere.

But no journal.

"You can take it in here," Molly told him. She waved her bandaged hand at the phone on the desk. It was barely visible for the piles of books surrounding it.

She'd protested his insistence that she sit on the chair and supervise while he continued the dusty work of unpacking and sorting. But he'd prevailed, and the white gauze on her hand was as pristine as it had been when they'd left Whitehorn.

He hadn't managed to get her to open up in the least about herself, but he did keep her from overtaxing herself after nearly slicing off the tip of her finger. And he'd kept her busy talking about Harriet. About a million little things that went into the ordinariness of a simple workday.

Harriet, while loathing the dreaded computers, hadn't much needed one, being as intensely organized as she had been. She kept lists of everything.

There had been at least two dozen in her desk, all filed according to some method that made sense to Molly but not much to Holt.

But there were no personal items included on the lists. No doodled hearts with "Harriet + ???" written in the center. Though frankly, Holt had a hard time imagining the no-nonsense Harriet doodling lovey-dovey stuff no matter what the circumstances.

Molly also pretty much confirmed the fact that while Harriet wasn't the most popular woman in town, neither did she have people who out-and-out disliked her. No angry library customers. What could she have done to anybody, anyway? Taken away their library card?

But his picture of the woman was deepening. Harriet had possessed a kind heart and a brusque tongue. She'd reeked of sensibleness, yet there'd been a romantic heart beating beneath her starched white cotton blouse. It was obvious in every single thing she did, every single person whose life she touched.

And still no journal.

"Holt? The phone call?"

Right. He wiped his hand on his pants and reached for the phone, hastily putting out a hand to stop a tower of hardcovers from sliding over. "Tanner, here."

"Don't you sound all gruff and official-like." Sue's cheerful voice greeted him. "There was an envelope in the afternoon mail today for you. I think it just might be that report on the tire tracks you've been waiting on. I figured you'd want to know right away."

"I did and you're a sweetheart. I'll be right there." He dropped the phone back on its cradle.

Finally. Maybe they were getting somewhere.

"Sweetheart?" Molly's eyebrows were raised a little.

She'd been all business since they'd returned from the clinic. Since he'd told her about Benny. "Jealous?"

"Not in the least. Particularly if 'sweetheart' gets you out of my hair for a while."

"Only as long as you're in the library surrounded by other people. The second you leave this place, you'll be accompanied either by me or the sheriff. For your own safety, of course."

Her smooth smile didn't waver. "Of course."

"I'll be back by five."

"Fine."

He didn't trust that breezy tone of hers for anything. "I mean it, Molly. Don't leave without me."

"Or what? You'll start a manhunt? It's a small town, Deputy. All you'd have to do, practically, is yell out the window if anybody's seen Molly Brewster, and you're bound to get a yell back in reply." Molly held her breath, suddenly afraid she might have overstepped the bounds of Holt's patience.

Particularly considering the way he just looked right back at her, all still and serious. "Smart-aleck."

She nearly choked. A nervous giggle wanted to rise in her throat, and she pursed her lips, containing it. "Cop."

His eyes crinkled and the faintest of grins touched his lips. And then he was gone.

Molly blew out a shaky breath, staring at her gauze-bundled finger. "What are you doing," she murmured.

"What's that, dear?" Mrs. English was standing in the doorway, her eyes kind.

Molly shook her head. "Nothing, Mrs. English. Would you mind rolling one of the carts in here so I can start moving some of these books out?"

"I'll bring one right over."

"Thanks." She chewed the inside of her cheek, eyeing the various piles of books. Most of them could be used in the bookmobile, she thought.

From the corner of her eye, she saw a movement outside the window, and looked out to see Holt striding across the street. She sighed faintly. The man really did have a way of moving that garnered a woman's attention.

The book cart rattled as Mrs. English rolled it inside the door, and Molly quickly turned away from the window.

"These books, dear?"

"Yes." Molly wove her way through the stacks and began loading the cart with the other woman's help. "You used to teach at the high school, didn't you?"

"Twenty-two years before I retired."

"They keep a set of yearbooks in the library there, don't they?"

"Oh, my, yes."

She glanced at the stack of yearbooks that she'd been moving out of her way all day. From the desk to the floor to the chair. Now they were back on the corner of the desk. "Harriet had a bunch of different years, some missing, though. I thought maybe the school would want them."

"They might. Sometimes a year disappears from the school's collection. If they don't, you should put a high-priced sticker on them and make some money at your sale. People love looking through these old things.''

Mrs. English picked up the top book and flipped it open, smiling as she paged through it. ''The school does have a fine journalism department. They always did put together a good yearbook. It's funny seeing some of these old faces. Look, here. That's Callie Griffin. Well, Sullivan, now. I keep forgetting that.'' She held out the book for Molly, then turned to the full cart. ''I'll just roll these out and start cataloging them, shall I?''

''Thank you, Mrs. English.''

The woman dimpled and trudged off with the rattling-wheeled cart.

Molly sat down in Harriet's chair, looking out the window again. She wondered what Holt's high school pictures had looked like. If he'd been as somber then as he was now, or if he'd let his humor freely show back then, before he'd had a cheating wife and held a dying partner.

Sighing a little, she paged through the yearbook, then reached for another. And another. In many of them she found photographs of Mrs. English, head of the—drum roll please—English department.

Photos of familiar people. Familiar places.

She smiled over Dee Dee Reingard's senior picture. Only, she'd been Dee Dee Durke back then. But still, the woman's face was identifiable in the pretty teenaged girl. ''Poor Dee Dee,'' Molly murmured. ''Dee Dee D.'' She shook her head and was still poring over the yearbooks when Mrs. English came back for another load of books.

"I told you they were fun to look through," Mrs. English said.

Molly reached for the last one. "There was a photograph of Henry Raines in one. I barely recognized him!"

"Oh, yes. Henry Raines was a good-looking young cuss. Frankly, he is five of the most boring people I know, so full of himself and being a past mayor. But back when he was a student, he had all the girls following after him. So did the sheriff. If a girl wasn't in love with Henry, they were in love with Dave Reingard."

"I haven't seen the sheriff's picture."

"Keep looking, then. I think he was a year ahead of Henry. You know that D.J. of his is a fine-looking young man, but his daddy, well, he was even better."

Molly found that hard to believe. She glanced at the year on the cover. The time was getting away from her, but she was curious now to see just how good-looking Sheriff Reingard had once been. Maybe if she could see more of his son in him, she could stop thinking about Rob every time she encountered the sheriff.

She flipped to the *R*s, and ran down the small group of students. There he was. She pursed her lips and whistled softly.

"Uh-huh." Mrs. English was back in the doorway, nodding. "I told you."

"Move over Robert Redford," Molly murmured, glancing at the printed names. "What? *Hiram?*" She laughed a little. "The sheriff's first name is Hiram?"

"Yeah, and my, did that boy have a fit when the yearbook staff put his whole name in there like that. I remember it like it was yesterday. Oh, he hated that name. David is his middle name—used it ever since I can remember. Only his mother called him by his given name, everybody else used his middle one.''

Molly's smile died a little. In her case, only her mother and Christina had called her by her middle name. Everybody else used her first one.

''Well.'' Thinking about her sister sobered her thoughts. For all Molly knew, Christina might well be a mother herself by now. She shut the book and rounded the desk to continue working her way through the mess of books. ''Mothers can get away with things like that, can't they.''

Holt found the large, flat envelope lying front and center on his metal desk when he got to his office. He sat down, glancing out the window at the library, thinking in a totally inappropriate way about how Molly had pursed those pink lips of hers.

''You going to read your mail or sit there drooling?'' Sue's voice was tart.

He shot her a look. ''Any luck with finding an officer named Rob Thompson?''

''Hon, there are seventy-nine Thompsons in the adjoining states. Give me a little time to narrow it down, why don't you? Maybe if you gave me a little more leeway on my search, I'd have better luck. Going about this from the back end instead of just contacting the PDs directly is a pain in the bu—''

''Just do it the way I said, okay? I've got my reasons.''

Sue's expression softened a little. ''I'll just bet you do,'' she murmured. ''Go on, then. Read your mail. Oh. I'll be able to pick up the enlargement of that picture sometime tomorrow. If we were in Whitehorn, we'd have one of those one-hour developing places, but here—"

"Tomorrow will be fine." He wasn't sure what he expected to find in an enlargement. Just a bunch of women, Molly included, clustered in front of Harriet's fireplace.

She'd looked pretty, Molly had. Her wavy hair curling around her cheeks, down for once. But it was the smile that tugged at him. She ought to have a smile like that on her face all the time. And Harriet, Harriet had been wearing a smile, too.

"Sue, how often did Harriet Martel call?"

"What? For the sheriff? A few times. Not very often."

"Did you ever hear her complain about trespassers?"

"Not to me. But then I wouldn't have. Harriet made it plain she wouldn't talk with anybody but the sheriff himself."

He hadn't expected to hear anything other than that. He tore open the envelope on his desk and pulled out the thin contents, forcing his concentration back to the report.

After he'd shot a roll of film on the three different tire tracks he'd found at the rear of Harriet's house, he'd taken castings of the tracks.

It hadn't been ideal that the castings weren't taken the same day Harriet's body had been discovered, but Dave hadn't put him in charge of the case until later. Still, Holt held out hope that the crime scene had been adequately preserved. In California they'd had an entire department to take care of the crime scene investigation. In Rumor, though, they had to do those kinds of things themselves.

The house had been sealed by Dave, broken only when Holt had gone in to do his own investigation of the place. And the property itself had been cordoned off as much as possible from curiosity seekers.

He glanced over the first page of the report, which mostly contained black-and-white reproductions of the photos he'd taken. The second page confirmed that one of the tracks belonged to Harriet's own car, which was about what Holt had expected. The second track was of the type issued with a particular late-model luxury car. And the third—

He shot back in his chair, staring at the results.

"Something wrong?"

He looked up at Sue. "Where's the sheriff?"

"Sitting outside your girlfriend's house watching it in case her intruder decides to come back. He's been there since first thing this morning, except when I went over for a while so he could take a lunch break. I thought that's what you wanted."

"It is." He pushed the report back into the envelope and headed for the door. "I'm going over there."

"To your girlfriend's house?"

He stopped and gave Sue a hard look. "She's not my girlfriend."

Sue smiled slightly. "Whatever you say, hon. Whatever you say."

Sue's words hung annoyingly in his thoughts as he headed to Molly's house. The sheriff was sitting right on Molly's porch, his boots propped on the rail, a book open on his lap and his head tilted back in a snore.

Watching the place.

Right. Maybe through his eyelids.

Holt nudged the sheriff's boot, and the man startled awake. The book slid to the ground. "What the hell?"

"What were your tire tracks doing in the back of Harriet Martel's house?"

Dave blinked, scrubbed his big palm down his face. "Damn, Deputy, what bug's crawled up your behind?" He planted his boots square on the porch and seemed to shake the sleep out of his head. "Now what's all this about?"

Holt tossed the envelope on the small iron table beside the sheriff. "Tires matching the type on your patrol vehicle left tracks in the rear of Harriet Martel's house. Pulled up close to the house. On the grass."

"So? I told you she was always calling me with complaints of trespassers." Dave looked irritated. He snatched up his book from the ground and thumped it on the table. "Of *course* my tire tracks were around there. Infernal woman wouldn't settle down until I'd drive out there and personally check out the place. Paranoid, I told you."

"In the grass behind her house?"

"She was weird about people parking in the front. Hell, Holt, anybody could tell you that. She once had to scrub an oil leak off her driveway, and complained about it for a month of Sundays. Everybody parked in the back 'cause nobody wanted to listen to her griping."

"You weren't parked in the back when you went out there after Molly called it in."

"Harriet was dead, she couldn't very well complain about it anymore, now could she." Dave stood. He wasn't as tall as Holt, but he was broader. And he was angry. "Just what are you implying, here? You think I had something to do with that woman's death?"

Holt stared at his boss. "I don't know what to think, Dave," he said evenly. "Seems odd, don't you think, that you never mentioned the castings I took might turn up as coming from *your* vehicle?"

Dave didn't blink. "Well, did your fan-damn-cy castings turn up anyone else's tracks?"

"A Mercedes."

"Henry Raines drives one, and he was her attorney. You gonna head on over there and arrest him for having the by-God nerve to park on his client's backyard? I told you those castings were a waste of time and effort, but did you listen? Hell, no. You're just some hotshot cop from California who thinks he's got all the answers us small-town folk are too damn dumb to learn for ourselves."

The hairs on the back of Holt's neck were prickling. Something wasn't right, and he knew it. But maybe he was getting as paranoid as everybody else was when it came to finding a dirty cop.

"Then why *did* you hire me?" His jaw was tight. God knows after the mess in California he hadn't exactly come with glowing references.

Dave picked up his book and the envelope and shoved them both under his arm. His face was red with heat. "Because you were the only one who applied. Now, either admit you've come to a dead end and put away the file on Harriet's case soon, so I can get the mayor and the rest of this town off my back, or I just might be forced to put out another help wanted ad. You get me?"

Holt watched Dave stomp down the steps. The

man stopped halfway down the walk and looked back. ''And by the way, just for good measure, I sent that lightbulb in for fingerprinting. The one that was burned out on the porch, there. Some citified genius didn't have the sense to check it out beyond mentioning it was burned out in the report. But I did, first thing this morning. We'll just see whether your little librarian is as paranoid as Harriet was, or if she just likes jacking you around for some attention.''

The sheriff strode over to his vehicle and drove off with a roar of the engine and a kick of dust from the tires.

Holt threw himself down on one of the uncomfortable iron chairs.

Great.

The day was turning out just…great.

Sitting there sulking wasn't going to accomplish much, Holt knew, but he let himself indulge for a brief while as the oppressive heat bored down on him. He was frustrated with the case, tired from a damn-near sleepless night on Molly Brewster's pain-in-the-back couch, and now, apparently, in danger of losing his job.

Well, so what was so different from living in California, after all?

Except there was no ocean within spittin' distance of his dinky apartment where he could forget his troubles for a while in the wash of aquamarine waves.

Instead there was an aquamarine-eyed woman he'd like to forget his troubles in, and there was no hope whatsoever of making that happen.

Chapter Twelve

"Here. I'm sorry it took me so long to repair it."

Holt glanced up from the newspaper to see Molly holding out his white shirt. It hung on a hanger, looking as spanking new as the day he'd bought the thing. He'd needed a decent shirt to attend his partner's funeral.

He supposed now he could wear it to a friend's wedding.

"Thanks." He took the hanger and ended up looping it over the back of his kitchen chair where he was sitting.

"Aren't you going to look at it? I don't think the tear is noticeable."

He didn't want to look at the shirt. He didn't want to look at Molly. It was Friday morning. He'd been under her roof for three nights, now, but it felt as if it had been centuries.

Sleepless nights and a perpetual hard-on did that to a man.

"I'm sure it's fine."

She huffed a little and padded, barefoot, over to the coffeepot, pouring a small measure into her prissy little white china cup. She was wearing a bright-yellow sundress today, and her hair was pulled up in its usual twist. The back of her neck looked soft as velvet.

Vulnerable as a baby.

He flipped to the sports section and stared blindly at it.

"Why don't you just go home, Deputy? There've been no more incidents here. It was probably just like the sheriff obviously thinks—my imagination."

"Is that what *you* think? That you hung your towels that particular way, that you arranged your pillows in that precise order?" He'd seen the way she hung her towels. Little ones on top of big ones. Two across. Always fresh, every day. The woman probably spent a fortune to own enough towels to change 'em the way she did, because as far as he could tell, she hadn't done any laundry since he'd been there.

"I don't know what I think anymore," she said, her voice charged with tension.

"Well then, let's just see what comes back from the lab on them."

"And what then? When they do come back, with nothing unusual on them, then you'll leave me alone?"

There *was* no sports section, he realized. Just an ad for a sporting goods store up in Whitehorn. He folded up the paper and tossed it on top of her briefcase that sat on one of the kitchen chairs.

She liked to take the paper with her to the library and read it in the middle of the morning when she took a break for peach yogurt and bottled water. And after she'd read it, she'd send it with one of the volunteers from the library over to old Barney Schoemaker, who sat in front of the general store every day. Barney, who liked to read the paper but was too cussed stubborn to pay more 'n a nickel for one like in the old days.

"I don't know," he said flatly. His answer was no better than hers, and it bugged him just as much.

He went to the counter, and she sidled out of the way when he reached for the coffeepot. He sloshed the rest of the pot into his mug.

She smelled fresh.

Cool.

If he didn't get fired, smelling sweet, close-mouthed Molly Brewster day in and day out was going to put him six feet under from sheer frustration.

She sipped her coffee. The massive amount of gauze on her finger had been rapidly replaced with a small adhesive bandage, and she seemed no worse the wear for the episode.

"You really are a crab in the mornings, Holt. You ought to see what you can do about that. Maybe you need—I don't know—more fiber or something."

Yeah, she might smell sweet as a spring morning, but there was nothing soft edged about her unexpected spurts of humor. The more time he spent with her, the more he was coming to realize it. Or maybe, the more she was just coming out of her shell.

Either way it was making her even more appealing to him.

Dammit.

"Molly," he said softly.

Her eyebrows rose. "Yes?"

His eyes focused on her lips. They were perfectly shaped. Not all bee-stung and pouty looking the way Van's had looked. But...perfect. Cupid's bow, he thought, wondering where the expression came from. Maybe one his grandfather had used.

He was losing his marbles, and the curiosity in Molly's expression was telling him so.

"Nothing." He shook his head. "Give me ten minutes. I'll take you to the library."

"My car is fixed now, remember? You followed me home from the garage yesterday after work."

"Like I said. Ten minutes. I'll take you to the library." Some things he could be flexible about. Not this. "Isn't Jupe coming in to take a look at Harriet's desk this morning?"

"Yes. He said he'll bring his pickup truck just in case he decides he wants the desk."

"And if he doesn't?"

"Then I'll have D.J. Reingard and his friends help move it out to the parking lot and maybe it'll sell next Saturday during the rummage sale." She tilted her head, her fingers toying with one of the little gold hoop earrings she wore. "I'm sorry, you know. I know you were counting on us finding Harriet's journal somewhere in her office." The office was all cleaned out, now. Nothing left save the ugly, over-size antique desk.

"Yeah, well, there've been a lot of things I'd hoped for, regarding this case, that have turned out to be dead ends."

"You'll figure it out."

"What's this? Faith from you? The queen of tight lips and no past?"

Her face whitened, and he felt even more vile than he had upon waking up on the floor that morning. He'd finally moved to the thin carpet from the hideous little couch out of sheer self-defense.

He exhaled roughly. "I'm sorry. That was uncalled-for."

"Even though it's true." Her movements were excruciatingly careful as she set her china cup and saucer on the countertop between them. "I know you think my ex-husband had a motive. But truly, Holt, Rob's anger was always directed solely at me. He was loud and…and frightening, but he wasn't really violent. Not physically."

"Except when he hit you."

She chewed her lip. "He was…disturbed when I left him."

"Disturbed enough that he'd break into your home and rearrange your stuff."

"It was to show his control over me." Molly's stomach was too tight suddenly for even the half cup of coffee. "That he could do what he wanted, go where he wanted, no matter how many times I changed my locks or whatever. He'd leave notes inside my locked car when I'd be out for the day, to show he always knew where I was, he—"

"—stalked you. And you think a guy like that would draw the line at murder," Holt scoffed. "Wise up, honey. Men who've had the object of their affection removed from them, for whatever reason, are capable of all sorts of nasty behavior."

"So what? We, the objects, should just put up with it?"

"No, I'm not saying that at all."

"Then what *are* you saying, Holt?"

"Tell me where he lives, so I can find out whether or not there's even reason to *think* he's a suspect. Molly, it's pretty obvious you'd like to rule him out as a suspect in Harriet's murder as well as being your home invader. Give me his whereabouts, and maybe I can *do* that!"

"If I do and you start looking into him, he will know it's *me* at the root of it, and whether or not he's had anything to do with what's gone on here in Rumor, my life here will be over. I'll have to find a new place to start all over again."

She swallowed, her eyes burning. "And you know what? I don't want to do that. I *like* it here. I love the people at the library. My reading groups. The honor-student group, the bookmobile project.

"I like walking through the park and watching the kids fly across the streets with their beach towels flapping, and I like knowing that most of the time, I'll see all of them sooner or later checking out a book or a video or coming in for the story hour. For the first time in my life, I'm doing something that I'm really good at! Something that matters to some-body else. Not playing the part of the soci—"

He closed his hands over her shoulders, pulling her around to face him. "The what? Society wife? Was your husband-the-cop also from money? Come *on,* Molly. Help me help you, before it's too late and I can't help either one of us. There's nothing written in stone that says you're gonna have to go anywhere. If this is the life you like, then this is the life you can keep. You've already proven you're tough enough to start over. You're sure as hell tough enough to hold on to what you've got!''

She couldn't breathe. Not with his big body so close to hers. Not with her hands resting on his broad, hard chest, the soft black hairs tickling against her palms.

Why, oh, why couldn't the man sleep in pajamas? Why did he have to walk around in those sweatpants? He seemed to have a half dozen pair. Gray. Black. Blue. And not a single T-shirt to be found along with them.

Her fingers curled against him, against that wonderfully warm, hard flesh, feeling the steady pump of his heartbeat. It was all she could do not to sway forward, not to rest her head against his shoulder and just…just…inhale him. ''Holt—''

He swore and let go of her so fast that she did sway. Her fingers curled against her palms, and she swallowed, feeling…bereft.

''Ten minutes,'' he said roughly, and pushed through the kitchen door so hard the thing bounced right back against the kitchen wall.

Her breath shuddered out of her lungs, and she leaned against the counter. It was either do that or just sink to the floor in a puddle.

From the back of the house she heard the rush of water when he turned on the shower. Every morning he said ''ten minutes'' but she knew it would be closer to six.

A few long breaths—in-two-three-four, out-two-three-four—later, she managed to take her cup and saucer to the sink, and rinse them without dropping them.

She cleaned the coffeepot, too. Dumped the

grounds in the trash and refilled it with fresh, making sure the timer was set to go off the next morning. She hadn't used the timer until Holt had come to stay, but he'd mentioned once that there was only one thing better than waking to the smell of coffee.

His wry expression had told her well enough just what he thought *was* better than waking to the smell of coffee.

Her hands shook as she gathered up her briefcase and went into the living room to wait. Two more minutes and he'd be striding down the hallway, buttoning up a fresh uniform shirt—he had them cleaned five at a time down at the dry cleaners—as he walked, his thick black hair slicked away from his sharply defined face.

Sometimes there would even be a glisten of water still on his eyelashes, making them look spiky and lending a ridiculous youthfulness to his thoroughly masculine face.

She hopped off the couch, stubbed her toe on the coffee table, and realized she hadn't even put on her shoes.

She'd been completely and utterly prepared to leave for work without her shoes.

A nervous laugh escaped.

"You're losing your mind Jolly Molly," she whispered. And felt such an incredible longing to call her sister that she actually picked up the telephone and began punching in numbers.

A rustle from the hallway caught her attention. Holt. His shirt half-buttoned over that ungodly perfect chest. Even as she watched, he tucked a white envelope under his arm and ran his fingers down to find the next button. He, of course, had on his shoes.

The nowhere-near-white tennis shoes that always made her want to smile. "Hey," he said. "I've got something I want to gi—"

"My name is Jennifer Molly Cannon," she blurted right over his words. "My sister used to call me Jolly Molly, which was such a joke, because she was the one who was far more jolly than I was. She h-had a million friends, and I h-had a million books."

He stood stock still, hands frozen on button and hole.

"Rob called me Jennifer, of course. It was so much more dignified than Molly. And image and dignity counted for a lot with him. Christina never liked him. She...she became my guardian when she was only twenty-two. Our...our parents died, you see. And I was still in school. High...school. And the authorities said I had to h-have a guardian, so Christina fought them all to do it. Because she loved me. We were always a t-team. Until Rob came along. And even after...she was there for me." She clutched the phone to her chest. "They l-loathed each other, but she never blamed me for all the trouble."

There weren't a lot of times in his life when Holt could honestly say he didn't know what to do. Yeah, times when his choices were more akin to the rock and a hard place, but times when he honest-to-God did not know what to do were few and far between.

This one, though, right now, watching Molly in her sunshine-yellow dress, looking as if her heart was breaking, clutching that phone between her hands as though it was a lifeline, he was at a complete loss.

He took a cautious step forward. "Of course she didn't blame you," he said.

"I miss her so much."

"Yeah. I...never had brothers or sisters. Benny was the closest thing I had to one, though. And...I miss him."

She fastened her gaze on him as if there was no tomorrow. "You're a loner."

"I suppose."

"People say that about me," she whispered. "But it isn't true."

"No."

Her throat worked. "Holt...I think I'm losing my mind."

He exhaled roughly, damning caution. He walked right over to her, peeling the cordless phone out of her white-knuckled grip, thumbing the disconnect to shut off the annoying bleating sound it was making, then tossing it onto the couch behind her. The envelope he'd all but forgotten under his arm followed the phone. "You're *not* losing your mind, Jolly Molly. The rest of the world may be going crazy, but you're not."

Her face crumpled, and it felt like someone reached down to his gut and twisted it with a grappling hook.

"I forgot to put on my shoes this morning." Her voice shook. "I had my briefcase in hand, was sitting here like a fool, waiting to leave for work as soon as y-you came out here. Is that the mark of a sane woman?"

He cupped her face in his hands, pressing his lips to her forehead, when all he wanted to do was crush her in his arms until she stopped shuddering. "Come on, baby, don't do this to yourself. It's been a tough month for everybody. Harriet's murder's been rippling around, having an effect on the entire town. Even you. Especially you. Stressing out a little is forgivable.''

Her hands tangled in his half-fastened shirt, and he choked down a groan.

''It was so awful, Holt. Finding her like that. I've never—''

''I know. Don't think about it.''

''I've *tried* not to think about it, and it ends up that is *all* I do! In my dreams I see her. Only then it's me sitting in that chair where I found her.'' She closed her eyes tightly, her lashes thick and black against her ivory skin. ''Or it's...it's Rob in the chair, and I'm standing over him h-holding the gun. What kind of a person does that make me?''

''Normal,'' he muttered, pulling her to the couch, sitting her down on the end where the broken spring didn't matter.

He pulled the coffee table over and sat on it, facing her. Holding her cold hands in his, tucking her trembling legs between his. ''Molly, finding Harriet the way you did was a traumatic event. And you've already lived through enough trauma because of your ex-husband. Naturally one thing set off stuff from the other. I'm not an expert, but I know you're just as sane as anybody else in this town is. But if it's bothering you so much, then find someone you *can* talk it over with. Angel Ramirez is qualified—''

She blinked, her head rearing back. ''What do you know about Angel Ramirez?''

He cursed himself. What was it about this woman that made him completely inept? It was no wonder he hadn't solved the case, he was too bloody distracted all the damned time. "I know about your trips to Whitehorn every Monday evening."

"You...what?"

"I know you go to a shelter for abused women every Monday evening. They have a group session at 7:30."

"And they have a literacy lesson at seven," Molly said evenly. "I teach it. That's *all*."

"Honey, there is no shame in it."

"I know there isn't. There is an appalling number of people who get through school without actually learning how to read—"

"Stop. You know what I mean."

Her eyebrows drew together. "Is that why you were so conveniently on the highway Monday night when my car broke down? Because you'd been following me?"

"I had to know what you were hiding. In case—"

"Yes, yes." She tugged her hands away from him. "In case it had something to do with Harriet's death. God knows that's the only thing we have in common. Harriet. Well, are you satisfied now?"

He stared at her. "You are the most confounding woman I have ever met."

"The only good thing I am to you is as a resource for Harriet's life. Or as a suspect somehow involved in her death."

He scrubbed a hand down his face, caught her with the other when she tried to move away. "The profile of Harriet's murderer was that of a man, Molly. Profiles can be wrong, and that's a stone fact, and I'm sorry if it offends you that we might have looked a bit closely at you. But statistics bear it out, honey.

The person that reports the body is often the person responsible for it.''

''But I didn't—''

''I know that. God, you can't lie worth squat, and I don't know why I ever thought you were the least bit like that.''

''My fingerprint, you took it, why did you take it unless some part of you still thought I was capable of—''

''Here.'' He picked up the envelope beside her and pushed it into her hands. ''There're your damn prints. All of them. From the glass, from your sink. Do with them whatever the hell you want, I don't care anymore.''

Molly's fingers tightened spasmodically over the envelope. He'd had the envelope with him when he'd been walking down the hall, buttoning his shirt. *Hey,* he'd said, *I've got something to...*what? *To give you.* Even before she'd lost her ninny mind and blurted all that out about her name and Christina...and her crazy-mixed-up nightmares concerning Harriet and Rob.

She was shaking. ''Why return them now?''

''Because Harriet isn't the only thing we've got in common,'' he said flatly. ''And you know it.''

Her lips parted. ''Holt—''

''We'll deal with that later,'' he said. ''Okay? Now listen to me. The profile of Harriet's killer. I want you to think about every single person she could have conceivably had contact with. I know we've talked about this for the past week, but, Molly, I'm running out of time.''

She frowned. ''Running out of time for what?''

He sighed mightily. "Are you gonna listen or ask questions."

"Okay. Okay."

"Male," he said. "Mature. Used to being in control. Probably drawn to positions of power, like a CEO of a company, maybe an elected official. Intelligent and charming enough to gain the trust of his victim.

"Whether or not that person was also the father of Harriet's baby, we don't know. But whoever it was had access and opportunity. We still can't conclusively set the time of Harriet's death between Saturday night or Sunday night, because of the high temperatures and humidity."

She looked ill. "Holt, I really don't want—"

"Sorry." He stood up and began pacing the room, his half-buttoned shirt billowing against him with each pivoting turn. "He left the crime scene, well, basically as clean as it could get. No hairs, no fibers, no signs of sexual contact, no fingerprints. He hit Harriet on the back of her head, near the neck, with a blunt object that we were unable to identify or locate. And he shot her at close range presumably through that missing pillow, with her own gun, leaving it to look like suicide.

"The guy knew what he was doing. If it wasn't premeditated, he managed to keep his head long enough to clean up the scene, to remove any trace of his presence." He stopped and faced Molly, shaking his head. "And if the sheriff finds out I'm telling you all of this, he probably will follow through with his threat and fire my ass."

"Ruprecht," she whispered. She stood, the envelope and little cards inside fell away from her lap to scatter on the floor around her bare feet.

''What?''

''Ruprecht Thompson. Mature. Drawn to positions of power. You're describing my ex-husband. Ohmigod, Holt, you are *describing Rob!*''

Chapter Thirteen

"Are you sure you're going to be all right here?"
Holt stood in the doorway of Harriet's office. "I
don't feel right about leaving you. I can send Sue
over to stay with you, or maybe Callie or Chelsea—"

"Chelsea is getting married tomorrow afternoon
to the mayor," Molly said. "And I'm sure Callie is
plenty busy with the lunch rush at the Calico. I'll be
fine." Now that she'd given Holt all the information
he needed to find her ex-husband, she felt curiously
calm.

Or maybe it was just numb.

She hadn't quite decided.

Holt still looked fit to protest, though. She could
see it in his dark eyes without him having to say a
single word.

"Nothing has changed since yesterday, or the day

before that, and you left me here at the library then, while you took care of your duties.''

''Yeah, well, that was before your ex-husband became the shortlist for Harriet's murderer.''

She shuddered. ''D.J. Reingard and the rest of the bookmobile kids are bringing by a load of stuff for the sale this afternoon. And I expect Mr. Jupe will be arriving any moment to give his yea or nay to Harriet's desk.'' She smoothed her hand over the top of the warm wood. Without the monstrosity of a desk in Harriet's office, her absence would seem even more final. ''So, go. Do what you need to do.''

Frankly, she *wanted* some time to herself, some time to think about everything that had happened, and definitely some time to gather her wits about her when it came to one Deputy Sheriff Holt Tanner.

What was wrong with her? It was practically a given now that her ex-husband had been involved in Harriet's murder. Which meant that if Molly had just had the courage to stay in Wyoming and live her life despite the torment Rob had brought to it, Harriet would still be alive today.

And what was she thinking about?

Harriet isn't the only thing we've got in common, he'd said.

We'll deal with that later, he'd also said.

She tugged at her earring, looking anywhere but at him. ''I, um, thought I'd call my sister, anyway. There's no point not to do so.'' And she needed to talk to Christina more than ever before.

''I'd rather you wait.''

''What? But why, when we know—''

''We *don't* know, Molly. We suspect. And until I

know more about your ex's current whereabouts, it'd be better if you don't change your habits now.''

She sank back on Harriet's desk, disappointment buffeting her.

''It shouldn't take long. He's a fairly high—'' He broke off hearing a commotion in the library.

A moment later Horton Jupe poked his head through the doorway, his eyes latching on to the desk with a gleam. ''What are you doing sitting on that thing with no respect for its antiquity?''

Molly hurriedly slid off the desk.

Jupe had already turned his attention elsewhere, however. He craned his neck upward, eyeing Holt up and down. ''One of the posts you planted tipped over,'' he accused.

''Why? You back into it with your truck and help it along?''

Molly pressed her lips together.

Mr. Jupe snorted and turned away from Holt in obvious dismissal. ''Well, I don't know how in blazes I'm gonna git that desk outta the doorway, but I guess I can be generous enough to take it off your hands.''

Over the old man's head, Molly saw Holt lower one eyelid in the moment before he left the office.

He'd *winked*. Holt Tanner had actually *winked* at her.

Bemused, she stepped out of Mr. Jupe's way. ''I know the sidepiece can be removed,'' she assured. ''Because it tends to come loose, anyway. It was never part of the original desk, either. And we can probably take the legs off, as well, if necessary.''

Jupe waved his hand, shushing her. ''I know that, missy. The desk had to get *in* that way, too. Now, be a good girl and git my toolbox. It's in my truck. And send that English woman—the one with the purdy ankles—in with a handcart. I know you got one somewhere around here."

Molly hesitated. This was a man who was on the library's board of trustees. He was, in effect, one of her bosses. "You know, Mr. Jupe, I'm sure we can find some help for you to dismantle the desk. I could go across the street and see who—"

"You think I'm too old and decrepit to wrangle a few pieces of wood?" His voice rose. "Git the tool-box!"

"Horton Jupe, you stop yelling at Miss Brewster." Mrs. English stood in the doorway, her hands fisted on her generous hips.

The man flushed. Red rose right up his neck, splotching his wrinkled cheeks. Molly suspected that if he'd been wearing a cap, he'd have snatched it off his head to twist between his hands. "I'll be back with the tools," she said, and barely made it out of the library before the soft laughter escaped.

She found the toolbox, which did weigh a half ton at least, and hefted it up the steps and into the library where she quickly drafted one of the book carts as a helper. She rolled it over to Harriet's office where Horton Jupe was making a bad show of not staring at Mrs. English's ankles.

"This thing all empty?" He was opening drawers, slamming them shut again.

Apparently slamming drawers was not as detrimental to such fine antiquities as sitting on the top of it was, Molly thought wryly. "Yes. All empty."

"Good." Jupe crabbed over to his toolbox and lifted the lid, pulling out a screwdriver and a hammer that looked older than he was. Muttering under his breath, he rounded the desk several times, studying it from all angles, Molly supposed. Then, muttering a little louder, he sat down on the floor and disappeared underneath it.

Mrs. English crossed her arms, sniffing. "Horton Jupe, if you hurt yourself under there, it's going to be nobody's fault but your own."

"Prissy woman," his voice drifted back, sounding hollow through the substantial wood surrounding him. "Nice ankles and wears the kind of shoes women are meant to wear, but you're still as prissy as you were fifty years ago."

Mrs. English flushed. She turned on her heel—slender two-inch pumps—and hurried out of the office. "Awful man," she muttered.

"Thought you said this thing was empty."

Molly dragged her attention from the flustered departure of her favorite volunteer and looked at the desk. "It is."

"Well, no, it ain't."

She heard a thump, a curse, and then Horton's hand stuck up over the back of the desk. He slid a thin book across the top of the desk, and a moment later was scrambling faster than she'd thought possible, as the sidepiece tilted sideways with an awful moan away from the main portion.

Molly's hand shook. She slowly reached out for the book, sliding it toward her on the desk. "I went all through that desk a dozen times. Where was it?"

Jupe was huffing as he pushed to his feet. He brushed back the three strands of hair on his sunburned head. "Ah, these old desks. Always had secret drawers and hidey-holes. If the sidepiece hadn't been screwed on all wrong, you'd a' been able to see the little button that popped open the panel underneath. Women, you know. Were always writing things they didn't want their decent husbands finding.'' Paying Molly no heed whatsoever, he left the office, hollering for Mrs. English to bring him the ''dad-burned handcart.''

Since the enormous desk had undoubtedly been designed for a man, Molly managed to refrain from comment about the need for hidey-holes. She lifted the cover.

The first page was blank except for Harriet's name written in the careful script that Molly had seen so often during the months she had worked with her.

''Well, Harriet,'' she murmured. ''It really was here, all along, wasn't it.''

''What's that?''

She whirled, and the cover of the journal closed gently over the first page. ''Sheriff Rein...gard.'' *Hiram,* she thought hurriedly. And her nervousness immediately subsided. A little. ''Is there something I can do for you?''

''I saw Jupe's truck, and figured he was over here being too stubborn to ask for help. He's been yammering about taking Harriet's desk for a few days now. Ever since you suggested it to him, I suppose.''

''Oh.'' She managed a smile. ''Well, good. I think he will need help.'' Not all cops are bad, she reminded herself. ''Here.'' She held out the thin volume. ''This is the journal Deputy Tanner has been looking for. Harriet's journal. Probably won't help much since...'' Her voice trailed away. Since the murder suspect was her ex-husband.

He grunted a little, taking the book. "Thanks. I'll take care of it. Better move outta the way, now."

Hiram or not, Molly still didn't much care for the sheriff. Looking at him was too much like looking at Rob. So she was happy enough to go.

And she had plenty to keep her busy, just as she'd told Holt. Once the scuffling and cussing and grunting of moving Harriet's desk out of the library was done, and the familiar silence settled over the place again, it was soon interrupted by the arrival of D.J. and his pals, and Molly spent the rest of the afternoon in the back of the parking lot, helping to sort through the two pickup loads of stuff the youths brought.

Somebody—Becky, maybe, because she was practical enough to think of such things—had procured several shade awnings, and while Tiffany oohed and ahhed over D.J. and the other boys' efforts to put them up, the rest of them arranged the boxes beneath.

There was still a week to go before the sale, but they simply had no other place to store the items. It was all just too much for the storage room of the library to contain—not when it was already crammed with bicycles and old lamps, a computer and a fairly well-kept recliner.

Maybe Molly couldn't call her sister yet. But she felt a great deal of peace come over her as she worked alongside the teenagers, laughing over their nonsense, smiling even at Tiffany's woefully obvious efforts at keeping D.J.'s attention.

And when they'd worked as long as they could without dropping from the heat, she called it quits and suggested everyone head to the town park where they could cool off in the lake.

She hadn't intended to get dragged along, but that's what happened.

And that's where Holt found her when he finally broke free and went looking.

He spotted Molly's gilded head among the others immediately, and took a while to just stand there in the grass and watch as she tossed a beach ball around with the teenagers who were standing in the shallows, kicking water at each other as much as they were tossing the ball.

Some wore swimsuits, some were in shorts and T-shirts. And Molly, still in her sunshine-yellow dress, looked water-spattered and happy.

It was ordinary and normal and the kind of activities he'd expect on a hot summer afternoon in a town where the residents all seemed to watch out for one another.

He sighed.

Looks were deceiving.

The beach ball bounded over someone's head, and he jogged forward, catching it up in his hands.

"Hey, Deputy, throw it here."

"No, to me."

"To me!"

He ignored all the calls and walked out onto the dock where Molly was seated, dangling her bare legs in the crystalline water. He tossed the ball way up into the air and D.J. dove for it, plowing into the cute red-haired girl next to him who did the same thing.

They missed the ball, but came up sputtering and laughing. Much to the chagrin of a curvy, sulky-looking blonde on the other side of them.

Molly looked up at him, and the sunlight crossed her face, making her hair sparkle with gold lights.

He wanted to touch that shining hair. Keep her near, where her glimmer could warm the dark parts inside him.

"Hi." She squinted against the sunlight and tossed her hand up to shade her eyes. "How'd you find us?"

"I caught Mrs. English when she was locking up over at the library. She said you were down here."

"Cooling off. They'd worked long enough sorting and cleaning stuff for the sale." She batted at the beach ball when it came her way, but he could see the concern in her eyes. "You've found out something."

"Yeah. Come on. Let me take you home." He held out his hand.

She eyed his hand. "Just tell me."

"Molly, I'd really rather not."

She looked back at the crew of teenagers and sighed. "I suppose you're right." She placed her hand in his and it felt cool and soft. But as he tugged her to her feet, he knew she was anything but soft.

She was tougher than anyone should have to be.

She slipped into her sandals and said goodbye to the teenagers. And even though there was no reason for her to need his hand, he kept hold of hers, sliding his fingers securely around hers, as they walked back to his truck. It was almost as far to the street where it was parked as it would have been to cut across the park to her house, but Holt wasn't going to chance being without his rig anytime soon.

Not after what he'd learned late that afternoon.

"What's in the bags?" she asked the second he was beside her in the cab.

"Your pillows and towels. The book, too. Not that

I ever thought you needed much help in the taking control department.'' The back seat was full of the stuff, all contained in big white trash bags. Apparently Chelsea's call to hurry it along had done some good after all. "They came back this morning."

"And? Did the lab find anything?"

"Nothing that didn't belong on them in the first place. Sorry."

Her smile died. She reached out and adjusted the air-conditioning vent. "It just falls more in line with what Rob used to do," she said after a moment. "Have you...um...contacted him yet?"

He shoved the truck into gear a little harder than necessary. "Wait until we get home."

Her eyes searched his. Her teeth nibbled at her soft lips. "Holt?"

"It's going to be okay," he told her. And even though he had no assurance of that fact whatsoever, her expression relaxed.

She believed him.

She trusted him.

The damnable thing was that he'd started trusting her, too. And now he was going to put information into her hands that would set her free.

And he'd lose her. No matter how much she claimed to like her life in Rumor, her reasons for being there no longer existed.

"All right, then," she said softly. "Let's go home."

Chapter Fourteen

"All right. I'm sitting."

They were in her kitchen. Holt had managed to put off telling her his news by dumping ice into glasses and pouring lemonade—it really was the from-scratch kind, just as he'd suspected all along—over it. He'd drunk down one glass and was on a second, and Molly was starting to look just a hair irritated.

"Right." He set down his glass.

Molly felt her heart drop down to her toes. Holt's expression had never looked so dark. And that was saying something. Nor had he ever minced words before, but now he was obviously searching for them.

He tucked his thumbs in his front pockets. "I know how hard it was for you to tell me about your ex-husband. Who he was."

"Yes," she admitted softly. "But if I'd just told

you right from the start about him, this would all be over.''

''Not exactly.''

''You've found him then.'' Her stomach jolted at the thought. ''Talked to him. And he has an alibi. Naturally. You can't just believe what he says, you know. Lying is as easy for him as breathing. He's a consummate manipulator.''

''Well, he wasn't lying this time.''

Molly shook her head, standing up. ''You can't be sure, Holt. You don't know him the way I do. You don't what he's capable—''

''I do know.'' He pushed her gently back down onto the hard kitchen chair. ''He's dead, Molly. Your ex-husband is dead.''

Molly blinked. Her vision narrowed, focusing only on Holt. On his brown eyes, the rich, soft-as-melted-chocolate brown eyes with the intriguing web of lines fanning out from the corners.

Her head felt oddly hollow.

''What did you say?''

He crouched down in front of her, his hands warm and strong where they rested on her knees through her damp yellow sundress.

Only she couldn't really feel her knees.

Because she'd gone curiously numb.

''He's dead. He was killed in a six-car pileup outside of Casper, Wyoming, three months ago.''

''Three…months.''

''Yes. A drunk trucker jackknifed his rig right in front of Rob's car. He didn't have a chance. The accident made half the newspapers in Wyoming, it's a wonder that some of the news wires didn't pick it up and make it here, too.''

Her throat felt tight. Raw. "Then Christina would know."

"She probably would."

"But if he's...gone, then who was in my house Tuesday night?"

"That's a good question," he said grimly. "And I intend to find out."

"Are you sure? He's, he's really dead. It's not some insane trick of his, some plan to smoke me out. He promised, Holt. He promised that he would never let me live in peace, that he would always f-find me, no matter what I did, he'd make me sorry for leaving him, he'd—"

Holt slid his arms around her, pulling her against him, tucking her head beneath his chin. She was trembling like a leaf.

"I'm really sure." Her hair was silky beneath his lips. "The local police there faxed the reports from the accident. I saw them myself. There were photos, honey. I'm really sure."

Her hands came around his back, and she was suddenly crying, great jagged sobs that caught at him, making him want to take away her pain.

She slid off the chair, and he held her still, right there on the faded linoleum floor in the small kitchen of a house that was less than a third of the size of the stately home she'd walked out of as Commander Ruprecht Thompson's pretty young wife three years ago.

His shirt got wet, his legs went numb, and still he held her. Smoothing back her hair, murmuring words that had no meaning, just letting her cry out all the years of pain and fear and solitude that a man who'd sworn to protect and serve had caused.

Until finally she lay against Holt, spent, only a hiccupping sigh left to occasionally ripple through her slender body.

"I have to call my sister."

He closed his eyes hard against the unfamiliar burning behind them. "She's away," he told her, wishing he could give her the answer she'd most want to hear. That she could rejoin her sister right now. And he was more selfish than his ex-wife had ever accused him of being, because he was glad that Molly wouldn't have an immediate reason to leave.

And leave she would. They always did.

"As soon as I knew Thompson wasn't a threat to anybody anymore, I had Sue contact Christina."

"But you didn't even know her last name. She's married—"

"I knew your name, Molly. That's all I needed. Your sister and her husband are on an African safari, if you can believe it. They're due back in a few weeks."

Molly was shaking.

"I'm sorry, honey, I can try to locate her. Fly you over there or something, but—"

"No." Molly tilted back her head, her eyes shining. "She always wanted to go on safari." She wiped her cheeks. "It was her biggest wish. She'd worked and saved all her money in high school and college to go, had the trip all planned—before our parents died. I...was a senior in high school, and she canceled her trip to stay with me. But she never stopped wanting to go. And now she has."

She scrambled back, and Holt's hands, empty of her, slowly lowered. "I can wait a few weeks," she said, her eyes flooding all over again. "I thought I'd have to wait a lifetime." She sniffed, looking away as she wiped her cheeks. "I got you all wet. I'm sorry."

He handed her his handkerchief. "I won't melt."

"No. I don't suppose you would." She smiled faintly, and wiped her face again, this time with his handkerchief. Then her smile faded. She looked down at the square of white fabric between her fingers. "You must really think I'm the world's biggest coward."

"What I think," he said quietly, honestly, "is that you are one of the smartest women I've ever known. Between you and Harriet, you managed to elude a man whose power stretched pretty damn far. You didn't submit to him, you didn't just take it. You took control of your life, and you left him and his obsessive behavior behind."

"I *ran* from it." She shook her head slightly and looked up at him. "Harriet helped give me the strength to run from it."

"All she did was give you a job, Molly. The rest you did yourself."

"Maybe. But it was still running." She wiped her face again. "You've helped me even more than she did."

"Me."

She caught her lip between her teeth, and he watched her visibly control her trembling. And he was so damned proud of her he wanted to cheer.

He wanted to take her in his arms and he wanted to kiss away every single tear she'd ever cried because of that bastard who'd hurt her.

And he wanted to hold her long enough that she would never go away.

But then, that'd make him no better than the man who'd made her life a misery for too many years.

"You," she said with a nod. "Harriet helped me escape my past. But you...you helped me to finally face up to it. And I'll never be able to repay you for that."

"There's nothing to repay, Molly. You'd have done this sooner or later all on your own."

"I don't think so," she said huskily. "Tuesday night when we came home from the Calico, and the park, and found my door unlocked, I was ready to run, all over again. I would have, if you hadn't been there."

"Well, it doesn't much matter. I was here. You didn't run. Thompson is never going to be a threat to you again, and I need to go." He dragged his legs up and pushed to his feet, which felt like they were being attacked by a million fiery ants.

Her eyes widened. "Oh...but, I—"

"Sue Gerhardt is going to stay with you tonight. Just for extra precaution, since we still don't know who broke in here. She's our dispatcher, but she's also an expert markswoman, and you'll be perfectly safe."

"I know who Sue is."

"Yeah. Right. Of course you do." His brain was turning to oatmeal. "I'll go gather up my stuff, then. It'll only take her a few minutes to get here once I call."

Molly stared as Holt strode from the kitchen, the door swinging back and forth madly behind him. "But I don't want you to go," she whispered.

The house was silent, completely so. Except for

an occasional thump. His boots, probably. Being shoved into that ratty gym bag of his.

Then she heard the rattle of the shower curtain hooks, and she knew he'd be reaching across the tub, grabbing the shampoo he'd bought because, as he'd told her, it was fine for her to smell green-apple fresh, but on him, he ended up feeling like a fruit salad.

She scrambled to her feet, pushing through the door that was still moving from him, and headed for the hallway, nearly skidding to a stop when he appeared at the other end.

"I don't want Sue," she said before she lost her nerve. "I want you."

His thick lashes kept her from seeing his expression. "Molly, it's not a good idea."

"It was a good enough idea earlier this week."

"That was before—" He shook his head, his jaw tight. He slung the strap of his bag onto his shoulder and headed for her.

But Molly stood her ground, blocking his way. "Before what?"

"Nothing. Would you move? I've gotta get my gun cleaning kit. I think it's still in the kitchen."

His stuff was all over her house. And she'd discovered that she liked it that way. "Before *what*, Holt?"

"Dammit, Molly. Trust me, this is not where you want to go."

"I want *you* to stay with me." There. She'd said it again. And it was easier the second time around. "You, Holt. Not Sue, who I know is a very nice and competent woman."

He took a step to the side, but she did, too. And

unless he was going to physically lift her out of the way, he was well and truly blocked in the hallway. ''Molly.''

''Is the couch *that* uncomfortable?''

His teeth bared a little. ''It is when the bed is where I want to be.''

She swallowed against the jolt that rocketed through her. ''Then you can have the bed.''

''God almighty, woman. Are you that naive? I don't want the *bed,* unless you are *in* it. And *that* is the reason why Sue Gerhardt is going to be staying with you, instead of me. Now move out of my way.''

''So then I'll be in it!''

''Molly—''

''*God almighty, man.* Are you that dense? I've just told you I want to sleep with you, and all you can say is 'Molly'?''

''I know you say you always pay your debts. But this is not the way to repay me.''

''And you said there was nothing to repay. Look, Holt, if you don't want me, if I've just imagined the—'' words failed her and she waved her hand ''—you know. Then say so.''

''You haven't imagined anything, and you know it.''

''Then why are you still holding your gym bag and looking ready to race out of here?''

''Because, dammit, I don't want to hurt you.'' He reached out and picked her right off the ground, moved past her, then set her back down before he disappeared into the kitchen again.

She darted over to the front door, slamming it shut just as he came out, his gun cleaning kit in his hand.

He sighed, looking thoroughly aggravated. "Again?"

"You're not going to hurt me."

"Molly, you— Dammit." He lowered his head, turned in a circle. Tossed down the kit where it bounced on the couch. "I know about your trips to Whitehorn every Monday night. I know where you visit. I know how Thompson treated you."

Molly pressed her lips together. "I thought we cleared this up already. I do some literacy tutoring there, as well as keep a reading group going for some of the women who've been there...well, a long time. And I have...gotten as much out of helping the women there as I've given.

"And maybe I do have a way to go before I can put all of the past completely behind me. But I'm not afraid to be with you, Holt. Don't you see? Yes, I want Harriet's killer found, you *know* I do. I thought we'd taken care of that when I told you about Rob. But the main reason I told you about him at all was because I couldn't be with you the way I want to be with you while that secret was hanging between us!

"Do you know what it's like?" Her hands lifted beseechingly. "To know you were sleeping out here on that horrible little secondhand couch, night after night, only a few feet away, and not be able to come out to you? To talk to you, to touch you—"

His gym bag hit the floor, and her back was suddenly pressed up against the door. "I don't have any gentleness in me for you, Molly," he said roughly, his body hard against hers. "And that's what you deserve."

Her breath stalled in her throat. She wriggled her hands free and touched his hard, tight jaw.

Gentleness, indeed. The man was made of the fiercest gentleness she'd ever dreamed of, and he didn't even know it.

"It's what we both deserve, Holt." She smoothed her thumb across his lower lip, choking down a moan when his eyes closed. He caught her hand, holding it to his lips, and pressed a kiss to her palm. "Please," she whispered. "Stay with me."

His eyes, when they opened, seemed lit with a golden flame. "You've had a shock today. Opening yourself up to the threat of your ex-husband again. Finding out he's dead."

"And that means I don't know what I want? I'd be the worst kind of hypocrite to say I'm sorry about his death. If I feel guilty over anything at all it's for feeling so relieved that I wasn't the cause of Harriet's death."

"I'd be taking advantage of the situation," he said doggedly.

She slid her hand around his neck, tugging his head lower until she could reach his ear. "Take advantage of me," she whispered. "We'll both have a lot more fun."

A strangled laugh came out of him. "You're a witch."

She couldn't help but fit her body against his. Not when his hard body barely gave her room to draw breath for the way his weight was pressing her against the door. "It's us quiet types men have to watch out for. Didn't your mama ever tell you that?"

He groaned and caught her hand from slipping under his shirt, and pressed it back against the door.

"The only thing my mama taught me was to stay out of sight when she brought some new guy home. Dammit, Molly," he grabbed her other hand, shackling it, too. "You're killing me. Don't you see? I have no control when it comes to you."

"I don't want you to be in control," she whispered baldly. "I've had enough of that to last a lifetime. There was nothing Rob did that wasn't controlled, thought out, planned." She'd been foolish enough to let the man sweep her off her feet, but she'd paid a high price for it.

"Rob chose my friends and my hairstyle. He put up with my work at the library only after he got on the board there. He dressed me to suit him, let me speak when it suited him and came into my separate bedroom when it suited him, which—as it turned out—was fortunately rare. And if I didn't suit him, he yelled. Where nobody could ever overhear him, he yelled. And then he hit me. So I left. I left him right in the middle of a party he was hosting. I walked out with a bunch of his guests and moved in with Christina, who opened her door to me without a question even though she wasn't one of the people in my life who'd *suited* Rob."

"Molly—"

"No." She twisted her hands around until she was holding Holt's wrists. "You might as well hear it, and then we can be done with it, I hope. After I left him, Rob stalked me. There. I've said it. But he didn't do it out of love, out of uncontrollable passion, some weird plan to romance me back into his life by some grand displays of obsessive behavior. He did it because he needed to be in control, because he wanted the power back. Power he'd lost the day I divorced him, so he took up a new tack with the break-ins. The notes. Because he had to prove he had more power than me.''

She stroked her thumbs against Holt's wrists. Such hard, inescapably masculine wrists belonging to a man who could turn around and help a kid who'd hurt him. ''The way Rob was, the way our marriage was, had nothing to do with *this*. With intimacy. Or passion. You *have* to see that, Holt.''

His hands slid up her arms, cradling her shoulders. ''I don't want to hurt you.''

Molly pressed her forehead against his neck. Right in that spot, that curve that seemed made just for her. ''You keep saying that,'' she whispered. ''Maybe I should be telling you that I don't want to hurt you.'' She suspected that he'd been hurt a lot in the past.

He stepped away from the door, and she nearly cried out at the loss of feeling him against her.

''Yeah. Bitty girl like you is gonna hurt me.'' He sounded amused, and she followed his lead.

''I don't know, Holt. It has been a while.''

She'd surprised him. His laugh was short. More an exhalation of surprise than anything else.

''Quiet types.'' He shook his head. ''This is not what I intended.''

''Ever?'' She took a step forward until her temple brushed his jaw. Until she could slide her fingernail down his shirt, circling one button after another. ''I don't think I believe that. Would it help if I tell you what to do? Put your arms around me.''

He did. His hands slid down behind her, fingers splayed so that if she closed her eyes and concentrated the slightest little bit she could make out each long finger stretching wonderfully from shoulder blade to shoulder blade.

"Don't poke the dragon too hard," he murmured. "You may get more than you bargained for."

"Promises, promises."

His hands swept from her shoulder blades down to her waist. Beyond. "You do have a wicked little streak in you, don't you, Jolly Molly."

Exhilaration swept through her. "Only with you, Holt."

His lips tilted. And his hands slid a few inches lower, curving about her hips, pulling her up tighter against him. "I guess it seems fair, since I'm the one you feel compelled to argue with most of the time. But trust me, honey." His breath was warm, intoxicating, along her jaw. Her earlobe. "It may have been a while for you, but you're 'while' ain't got nothing on the torture of watching you every morning peek out your bedroom door to see if I'm still asleep, then tiptoe across to the bathroom, almost soundlessly close the door, then proceed to hum golden oldies while you shower."

Her head reared back. "You could hear me?"

His gaze fastened on her mouth. "Yeah. Hear. Imagine." He lifted one hand, slid his long fingers along her jaw, running his thumb over her lips. "I'm telling you. Serious torture."

She kissed his thumb. "Poor baby."

A flame burned in his eyes. "Molly. I can't joke anymore about this. I don't have it in me."

Her heart in her throat, Molly stepped back, sliding her hands down his arms, linking her fingers through his. "You won't hurt me," she whispered. "And I'm not laughing."

She wasn't scared, but she was shaking as she turned and headed down the hallway to her bedroom, her hand tightly on Holt's. And then they were in her bedroom, her unimpressively sized bed seeming larger than life right there in front of their faces.

"God in heaven you are going to kill me," he whispered, mistaking her hesitation for...hesitation. "Say no now, Molly. Say it, and I'm out of here. I may go throw myself off a cliff afterward, but—"

"I thought you couldn't joke anymore."

"Who's joking?"

And just that easily, Molly's tremors slid from her shoulders to deep inside her, causing an altogether different type of reaction. "Can't be you," her fingers tugged at the buttons of his shirt, "because everyone knows that Holt Tanner is always serious."

Her heart did an odd jig in her chest when he shrugged the shirt off his shoulders. Then his arms came around her, pulling her close. And his mouth, oh, yes, his mouth finally found hers, fierce and heated. He pushed the straps of her dress free, and their hands fumbled together as they tried to free the little zip in the back. And still he kissed her. And she kissed him back. The way she'd thought of that day so long ago in the hardware aisle, before she'd known who he was, before either one of their guards went up.

Someone was moaning a little, she thought it might be her, and they gave up fighting her dress as Holt tipped her onto the bed.

"Hurry," she whispered, begged, when he stopped to deal with his belt, those California-boy tennis shoes. She shifted restlessly, wanting his weight, wanting his everything, her hands lifted to him, ready to tug him back down to her.

But he eluded her, grabbing his pants again, muttering under his breath, making her smile and grin and want to laugh for the sheer freedom and joy of being with him.

Then he was back and his palms slid against hers and the bed dipped under his weight. He pressed her hands to the bed and pulled the clip from her hair, threading his fingers through it until it spread out in waves about her head.

"You're perfect," he said.

She murmured his name, and his eyes crinkled, and again she wondered how she could ever have thought him to be so grim. She touched his jaw, his neck, his shoulder. "So are you, Holt," she whispered. Her skin tingled wherever he touched, and she shifted restlessly against him, sliding her leg along his, loving the rougher feel of it against hers. "I want to be perfect together."

He let out a long breath, as if even then he'd been prepared to stop if she gave the slightest hint that she wasn't ready for this. His lips found hers, and then his hands were racing over her, only to pause and linger, not the least bit hindered by the dress tangling about her waist as he pushed their torment two hundred degrees higher.

Until her hands scrabbled at his strong hips; until she pulled him over her, mute gasp on her lips, aching want in her soul; and she took him in, where neither would ever feel lonely again.

And after, while their hearts still pounded in their chests, while he was still a part of her, he turned on his back, pulling her over him, cradling her face in his hands, eyes searching hers, before he pressed his mouth to hers.

He kissed her, so beautifully and so full of gentleness that the tears that had already collected in the corners of her eyes overflowed.

"You lied," she said quietly. "All that you have in you is gentleness."

He smiled faintly, brushed his thumb down her cheek, following the line of tears. She slipped down beside him, his arms holding her close, her hand sliding over his chest until she could feel the steady bump of his heartbeat. And then, exhausted and satisfied, they slept.

Chapter Fifteen

"So what happens now?"

Holt looked at Molly, his gaze pausing over the soft vee of skin showing between the lapels of her robe. They were on her bed still, where they'd managed to "while" away the entire evening and half the night. Only more-practical hunger had rousted them from the tumbled bed, but they'd still returned quickly enough.

And there he lay, a plate of tortilla chips and melted cheese sitting on his belly. "Well, the spirit is willing, honey, but I'm not as young as I used to be. And three times in—"

"Oh, hush." Her cheeks pinkened, and he smiled faintly.

There weren't many women he knew who blushed, and sure in hell none who could turn him on while doing it, except shy Molly Brewster.

Who wasn't so shy after all when it came to certain things.

"I *meant* about the case."

He bunched up the pillow under his head, then dropped his hand back to her knee. She was sitting cross-legged beside him, the robe tucked primly all about her. Except for that slice of skin between her breasts and the knee he'd unearthed from all that terry cloth.

He did have a thing for her knees.

He had a thing for her, period, end of story.

"Lenny Hostetler moves to the head of the class," he said. He picked a chip, breaking off the string of melted cheese that clung to it, and popped it in his mouth.

"What about Harriet's journal? Did you read anything helpful in it?"

The chip lodged in his throat, and he sat up sharply, coughing. "What?"

"The journal. The sheriff gave it to you, didn't he?"

Holt shoved the plate of chips on her nightstand. It knocked against the small stack of books there. "You found Harriet's journal?"

"Well, I didn't. Mr. Jupe did, actually. When he was taking apart the desk. Apparently there was some sort of hidden—"

Holt was already heading down the hallway, looking around for the phone. It was under the leg of the couch. He dialed Sue's number first. At least with Sue he had some chance of getting a straight answer.

He didn't know what to expect from the sheriff these days, except maybe Holt's walking papers.

"Did Reingard log in any evidence today on the

Martel case?'' he said the minute the phone was picked up.

"Good evening to you, too, Holt.'' Sue's voice was groggy. "Do you know it is two in the morning?''

"I'm sorry.'' He wasn't. "Did he?''

"Yes. Well, I'm not positive, actually. But I saw him writing out an evidence tag as I was leaving for the day. Why, what's wrong?''

Holt sighed. If Dave had logged it in, then it was unlikely he was trying to hide something. "Not a thing, Sue. Just looking for a thread.''

He hung up and turned to find Molly watching him. "Get dressed,'' he said. "I want to read that journal, but there's no way I'm leaving you alone.''

She didn't argue. Two minutes later they were both dressed and making the short drive over to the sheriff department. The journal was right where it should be, logged in as official as you please. "You know,'' Holt said, as he logged it right back out and handed the oversize bag to Molly, "if I actually manage to make an arrest on this case without Dave taking me off it, or him firing me altogether, it's gonna be a miracle.''

"Why would he fire you?''

"Don't think he much appreciates my citified ways,'' he muttered. "Either that, or my reputation has managed to follow me a little too well.''

"What reputation?''

He ushered her from the office and relocked the door. "Two o'clock in the morning isn't a real bad time of night.'' He tilted his head back. "Think it's actually…nice outside.''

She tucked her hand in his arm and pulled him back to his SUV. "*What* reputation?"

He tossed her the journal. "Are you going to go with me to Chelsea and Pierce's wedding tomorrow. Today?"

"Holt, *stop*...really? You want me to go with you to the mayor's wedding?"

He looked over at her. Her hair was loose, tumbling around her shoulders in mad waves as if she'd just climbed from bed. Which she had. He was pretty sure the orange shirt she'd pulled on was inside out, too.

She was beautiful.

If the back seat of his truck weren't still taken up with the pillows and towels sent back from White-horn, he'd have seriously considered tugging her back there right then and there.

"Why wouldn't I want to take you?"

"Well," she plucked at the edge of the clear bag containing the journal. "That would be kind of like a date."

"What? I'm good enough to sleep with, but not to date? I'll shower and brush my teeth, promise."

"You know that's not what I mean."

He dropped his left wrist over the steering wheel, looking over at her. "The advantage of bench seats," he observed, "is this." He closed his other hand around the side of her denim shorts and pulled, sliding her right over beside him. "Half this town already thinks you're my girlfriend," he said.

Her eyes widened. "They do not!"

"Trust me. Sue's been making noises about it for days. She may be tight-lipped about what goes on at the station, but when it comes to gossip like that, she could sink a ship with those loose lips."

"And you like her."

He shrugged, finally turning the ignition and heading back to Molly's place. "Yeah. She reminds me of Joy. Benny's wife."

Molly watched his face in the dim light from the dash. "The one who gave you the tie with the surfers on it."

She caught his faint smile. "That'd be her," he said. "She's the one who saw the notice for the opening here in Rumor."

"Why'd you want to leave California? Because of your partner's death?"

"Close enough."

"Holt—"

They were already back at her house, and he parked in the narrow driveway, right behind her rattletrap sedan. "It's not all that interesting a story."

She didn't wait for him to come around and open her door, but joined him on the sidewalk. "I think everything about you is interesting."

"Well." He slid the journal out of her hand and walked with her up the steps to the door. "The only thing I'm interested in right now, other than you, is reading Harriet's hopefully interesting journal."

Molly was still reading it, aloud, as he drove them to the wedding of Chelsea Kearns and Mayor Pierce Dalton that afternoon. Harriet hadn't written in her journal every day by any means. The entries—touching on everything from Henry Raines's blessed unseating as mayor to heartwarming comments about her sister and nephew, Colby—spanned several years.

The most recent entries had seemed to come more regularly. And unlike Harriet's usual organized ways, some entries were dated but some were not. And they read rather like a romance. The excitement of that first kiss. The beauty of making love. And the guilt of it.

"You know—" she set the book in her lap for a moment "—Harriet really loved him."

"But even in her own journal she didn't identify her lover with anything other than an *H*."

"She mentions H's wife," Molly countered. "She felt bad for hurting her, even if it was unknowingly."

"Which leaves out Henry Raines, who's divorced, and not somebody Harriet wrote about in glowing terms, anyway. And Horton Jupe."

"Mr. Jupe!"

"He's a crazy old coot, but he's on the library board. He knew Harriet."

"And thinking about Harriet with him is enough to—"

"—make you lose your lunch."

She covered her mouth, muffling a laugh. "Well, maybe not quite that bad."

"Henry, Horton, Harold, Hugh." Holt shook his head. "And then there are those with the *last* name of H. Holmes—"

"Her brother-in-law? I don't think so."

"Well, as it happens, neither do I. Colby Holmes and I went through every name of every resident in the county, I swear, trying to match up the initials Harriet wrote on the back of that book at her house."

"Maybe it wasn't initials," Molly said again.

"Maybe she was trying to just write a word. What were they?" She remembered too late the way he'd kept silent on the information, before.

It seemed inconceivable that it had only been a few days ago. Not when her life had changed so much in such a short time.

"*H*," Holt said. "*I*. The last letter could be an *M*, maybe an *N* or an *R*. It was too smudged. If she'd had a pen or something to work with, but—"

"Him." Molly could hardly bear to think about what Harriet had endured in her last moments. "Hint. Hide?"

"That would have applied to you, maybe, but we've pretty effectively ruled out your ex. He was already dead."

"Well, Henry Raines is out." She went back to names. "No wife. Hostetler."

"I wish we could find good ol' Lenny. But I seriously doubt he was the lover Harriet wrote about."

"He was married."

"And Harriet helped his wife and kids get away from him to Boston. Besides, Lenny's type is pretty, young blondes, not forty-something brunettes."

"Does Lenny have any brothers? Other Hostetlers?"

Holt shook his head. He plucked the journal off her lap and locked it in the glove box. "Enough. I'm right back where I was four weeks ago. A lot of speculation and no physical evidence."

"If you could find the pillow that she was shot through?"

"Or whatever the killer used to hit her on the back of the neck, then maybe I'd be getting somewhere.

Come on. Look. There's a crowd over there already.''

Molly looked over, and just as Holt had said, there was a small number of people milling about the lovely grounds in front of the Blue Spruce Resort. ''Holt.'' She caught his sleeve. He was wearing the same suit he'd worn the day he'd come to the library. They'd stopped and bought him a new tie, though, on the way. One without surfers on it. ''There are only a few people here. Obviously, this was meant to be a fairly private ceremony.''

''With a few friends. Yeah. Come on.'' His gaze drifted over her. ''Did I tell you that you look beautiful? I really like it when you leave your hair down. Reminds me of the way you look lying back on those soft sheets of yours.''

Her face heated, along with everything else about her. ''But I'm not one of their friends. I'm not in that circle. I feel like I'm gate-crashing or something.''

''*Circle*. Trust me, honey, these people aren't snobs. My ex-wife and her rich friends were snobs, so I know. Pierce and Chelsea are good folk. And I am one of their friends.'' For one of the first times, he actually felt the truth of that particular word. It didn't have anything to do with something Chelsea or Pierce had said or done. It was something inside of him.

Something that was changing because of Molly.

''And you're my...friend,'' he said. ''You want us to drive back to the station so I can find the invitation to show you? It said 'Holt Tanner and guest,' I promise.''

She relaxed a little. ''You never mentioned your ex-wife had money.''

"I try not to think about it," he assured her dryly. "Money doesn't necessarily mean class. When it comes to that, you blow her right out of the universe."

Molly looked at him. "Holt—"

"It's true. After the novelty of marriage with the hardworking cop she claimed she'd loved enough to honor and cherish till death wore off, she went right back to her useless rich boyfriend." Saying the words didn't even hurt anymore. Vanessa had been...Vanessa. Knocking people over in her way to getting what she wanted, no matter what the cost, or who she hurt with her lies.

"I'm sorry." Molly stroked her hand over his jaw. "That must have hurt."

"Not anymore," he said. And knew it was true. "We, uh, could spend this afternoon doing something other than hobnobbing with the mayor, though, if you're really insistent on not staying."

She huffed, but he could tell she was tempted. "We're already here. And as you said, they're your friends. So, come on." She brushed her hands down her thin, floaty dress that managed to look innocent and sexy all at the same time, and they headed toward the small cluster of white chairs that were set out on the brilliant-green grass.

The rest of Montana might be drying up, but the Blue Spruce apparently had an unlimited water supply, Holt thought wryly.

There was a small quartet sitting off to the side, and they were already playing when he and Molly slipped into two seats in the last row. He was aware of Chelsea walking up the short aisle between the seats a few minutes later, but he was more interested in watching Molly.

Her eyes sparkled, and her pretty blond hair drifted around her face when a wave of air passed through. And Holt had the weirdest notion that he could hear Benny's gravelly laughter on that breeze.

Before he knew it, Molly was dashing tears from her eyes and tugging him to his feet, and everybody was crowding around the new bride and groom, offering their best wishes and congratulations. Everybody except Holt. He pulled Molly around, tugging her close, because he was a lot more interested in kissing her than he was the mayor's new wife.

So he did.

But nowhere near as thoroughly as he wanted.

He tried to cut their attendance at the reception as short as politeness would allow. Molly insisted that he actually speak to the new bride and groom before they left, though, so he pulled her along with him, not giving two figs what anybody thought about the deputy sheriff consorting with the woman who'd discovered Harriet Martel's poor dead body.

He kissed Chelsea's cheek and shook Pierce's hand and wished them the best of luck, and even managed to believe that if any two people could make a success of it, it would be them.

But Chelsea caught his hand, her eyes laughing, and tugged them down to sit at the table with them. "We're going on our honeymoon," she told Holt, "but I'll have my phone with me, so if anything comes up about the case—"

Pierce made a protesting sound, but Chelsea shushed him with a tart "You'd do the same thing, and you know it," and turned right back to Holt.

"So, if anything *important*," she added, "comes up about the case, you be sure to let us know."

So of course Holt had to sit there awhile longer telling the new bride and groom—who were no doubt as interested in starting their honeymoon as he was in getting Molly back to her soft-sheeted bed—about the journal and what it had contained.

Chelsea propped her chin on her wrist, looking thoughtful. If she thought Holt's choice of a date was odd, she kept it to herself. "We speculated that the father of her baby could be married. It's the perfect excuse why she kept the relationship secret."

"And you're pretty much back where you started, when it comes to suspects," Pierce said.

Holt tucked his hand over Molly's. "There's a loose thread somewhere. There always is. I haven't been back to her house since I got the case. Maybe I missed something. I managed to miss the hiding place in Harriet's desk."

"Only because of the way the return had been fastened badly," Molly said. "Mr. Jupe said the hiding place would have been noticeable then, when someone really looked."

Holt shook his head. It didn't matter what the excuse. He'd missed it. "I'm going to have to go back to the house. Start from scratch."

"I hate this business," Pierce said flatly. "Rumor isn't a town where people get murdered in their own homes. Where people get murdered at all."

Chelsea murmured sympathetically and leaned over to kiss her husband's cheek.

"Well," the mayor said abruptly. "Time to go." He looked at Holt. "You'll figure it out. I know that."

"Dave doesn't seem to think so."

"I told you I'd talk to him."

"That may be," Holt said, "but I think he just took it as more pressure to get the case solved or shelved." He stood, sticking his hand out again to Pierce. "Anyway, good luck to you both."

Molly smiled and wished them happiness, and Holt dragged her away, ignoring the muffled laughter coming from Chelsea and Pierce behind them.

Molly waited until they were nearly back at Holt's truck. "Why didn't you tell the mayor that the sheriff is threatening to fire you?"

"Men don't go whining to the mayor about crap like that. I can handle Dave." He yanked open the passenger door, put his hands at her waist and popped her up on the seat.

Her eyes widened, then softened, when he stepped between her legs. She looped her arms around his shoulders but gasped when his hands slid under the hem of her dress, cupping her knees.

"Holt Tanner!"

"Shh." His thumbs smoothed over her thighs. Climbing.

She wriggled. Toward him. Away from him. It was hard to tell. But her hands weren't letting him go anywhere, the way they were latched around his neck, sliding through his hair. "There are two dozen people over there!"

"Who can't see a thing on this side of the truck."

"We—" her mouth fell open, sucking in a quick breath "—*can't!*"

"Yeah." He blew out a noisy breath. "I know." He kissed her hard, and regretfully moved his hands to a more respectable location.

She rained little kisses along his jaw, seriously tempting that notion of *can't*. "So let's go back home," she said softly. "You can drive fast. Nobody's about to give *you* a speeding ticket."

Chapter Sixteen

"Don't touch anything."

"I know, I know." Molly stood behind Holt as he sliced through the flat yellow sticker proclaiming Harriet's house as a crime scene that was not to be disturbed. "I'm the camera holder," she said, trying for some levity.

She really, *really* did not want to go back into Harriet's house. Not that there was anything frightening about the house itself, she told herself, focusing on the green shutters and the pretty flower boxes in the windows.

But Holt had asked her to come, and so she'd come.

It was that simple.

She stared harder at the white house. The green shutters. "Somebody's been watering Harriet's plants."

"Probably Colby and Tessa Madison."

"The psychic."

He was working his hands into thin gloves. "I predict they'll be getting married."

Molly snorted softly. "You shouldn't scoff. In her journal, Harriet mentions the gold pen as a gift from 'H.' and you told me Tessa was the one who said there was something special about the pen."

"I know. She was on the mark about everything, and I wouldn't dream of scoffing." He began working on the second glove. "It's about time I got out here to do this again. The sheriff has spent the entire week putting me on everything from—"

"—Jupe's fence posts to traffic control. I know. I've hardly seen you since the mayor's wedding last Saturday."

"You've seen me at night," he murmured, and she flushed a little, far too easily distracted by him.

"Well, we're here now." She hefted the camera she was carrying for him and wiggled it.

"Right." He snapped the wrist of one glove and waggled his eyebrows at her. "Wanna play doctor?"

"Whoever thought you had no sense of humor was way wrong."

He grinned a little and turned back to the door, fitting the key in the lock. It opened smoothly. "Come on. And don't—"

"Touch anything. I *know*." Shaking her head, Molly concentrated on Holt's back as he stepped into Harriet's house. It was dark and warm and smelled musty from being closed up ever since—

"There are the matching chairs," Holt said.

And one missing the decorative pillow. Molly

lifted the big camera and handed it to him. He immediately began clicking off a few shots.

She didn't look toward the desk or the chair where she'd found Harriet. "Do you want me to turn on the light or something? Maybe open the drapes?" They'd left the door open, but it didn't help much. The sun was half-down, and it was overcast. "I wish it would cool off a little for our rummage sale tomorrow."

He moved over and took a photo of the fireplace. "Never know. It might. A lot can happen in a day."

She eyed him. "That's certainly true enough." Look at how far they'd come in only a few weeks.

His lips tilted, and he continued working his way around the room. Photographing this. Photographing that. She had no clue why it would be important to photograph the angle of the plant sitting by the front window, but he must have. He disappeared down the hallway, and she could hear the distinctive sound of the powerful flash.

She started to sit on the arm of the couch, but stopped and shook her head a little. Keeping her back to the desk and chair, she moved closer to the door again. "What's going to happen with all of Harriet's things?"

He came back down the hall and handed her the camera. "Once we've no longer got control of it as a crime scene? It'll be up to her sister to handle this part of her estate." He pulled out a thick file folder and moved over to Harriet's desk, opening it and laying it down there.

Molly looked away. He'd pulled out a tape measure and was walking around, taking measurements, noting them down in his small notebook, looking back at the file on the desk.

She stepped into the doorway again, breathing the fresh, nonmusty, air. "How long does it take before it doesn't get to you? Investigating stuff like this?"

He grunted. "I'll let you know when I reach it. I started out in Vice with Benny. Spent time with Crime Scene—that was a bundle of joy, I can tell you, but I learned some lessons well—homicide, a gang task force. None of it's pretty."

"Why do it, then?" She folded her hands beneath her arms. Not touching anything was a lot easier said than done.

"Nothing else I'm good at." She looked over at him again, seeing him straighten and toss the tape measure into the evidence kit he'd carried inside. He tore off one glove and ran his hand down his face. "Not even sure I'm that good at it, anyway."

"Why? Because you haven't been able to determine Harriet's murderer?"

He propped his hands on his hips, his attention on the desk. "I came to Rumor because I didn't want any more of this," he said roughly. "Cases that you know are gonna turn bad. This kind of thing isn't like a drive-by shooting or the like. That stuff's bad enough. Random violence by some kid proving his loyalty to his new colors. This is murder, carefully carried out…" He blew out a breath and scrubbed his hand down his face again. "God help me, but I'd rather plant a dozen posts for Horton Jupe or direct traffic in perfect-town, Montana."

Molly couldn't stand it. She moved over behind him, rubbing her hands over his tight shoulders. Even if it did mean standing three feet away from the chair where she'd discovered poor Harriet. "I have faith in you."

He turned around so fast she wobbled. "Why?"

She pressed her lips together. "Because I've always known you'd be the kind to uncover truths. Why do you suppose I was so determined to stay away from you?"

"Common sense?" Holt's lips twisted. He might have Jolly Molly at his side right now, but sooner or later she wouldn't be. Probably sooner. Like one week, when her sister returned to Wyoming from her safari to find the messages that had been left for her from Molly.

"Come on. I'm done here." He tucked his little notebook in his pocket and hunkered down to stuff the file back on the top of his kit and close it up. There was a half a pistachio shell lying on the carpet next to one of the legs of the desk.

Dave and his damned pistachios.

Holt shook his head and straightened, nudging Molly to the door. He locked it up again, plastered fresh tape across it and headed to his truck. "If we drive into Whitehorn right now, I can probably get the film developed today."

"Sure, whatever you ne—"

"Ah, hell."

Molly paused, waiting for him. "Holt? What's wrong?"

"I found a thread," he said.

"All right. Look here." Holt had spread a series of photographs across Molly's kitchen counter. "The top row are the photos from Harriet's place that Dave took when he responded on the call you made about her. The bottom row are the ones I took from today.''

Molly wiped the tiredness from her eyes and focused on the photos. It was well after midnight, and he knew she had to meet the kids at the library for the rummage sale in a few hours. But he needed a fresh pair of eyes.

''So, what am I supposed to be seeing?''

''Something…different.'' Holt shook his head. ''If I knew, I wouldn't have dragged you out of bed.''

On the window ledge above the counter, he'd propped the enlargement of the reading group photograph. Molly looked from that to the rows of photographs. ''I feel like I'm looking at one of those puzzles from the newspaper,'' she said. ''The ones where you're supposed to find six things different between two seemingly identical drawings.''

''I doubt there're six things,'' Holt said, ''but there's gotta be at least one.''

''Why are you so sure?''

''I just am. Now, look.''

She brushed her tumbled hair out of her eyes and picked up two photos, identical shots. ''Can I move these?''

''Go ahead. They're dated.''

She carried them to the table and sat down. She did the same thing he'd done. Starting at the top, reading across it like words on a page, comparing every aspect of one photo to the other. Finding nothing, she took the next two photos. And the next.

He rubbed at the pain between his eyes and drank another cup of too-strong, cold coffee.

''I think there's something different on the mantel.''

Holt dumped the coffee in the sink and went over to her. She pushed the rest of the photos she'd been looking at out of the way. "Look. Here's your first set. The candles. Harriet had at least a dozen burning on the mantelpiece the Thursday before she died. The candlesticks are all there in your photo taken after her death. See how closely they're pushed together? But in this one," she touched the second photo, "the candlesticks aren't standing so close to each other. They're more spread apart. I don't know. It looks to me like they've been moved."

"The wound on Harriet's neck didn't match any of the candlesticks."

"So, something else was on the mantel?" She picked up the first photo and peered at it. "What's the enlarged one look like?"

Holt grabbed it off the window ledge and laid it on the table. They leaned over it, looking. "This isn't any better," Molly said, sounding frustrated. "Miriam Hughes's head is in the way."

"I wish Helen had taken more than one shot that night, is what I wish." But he knew she hadn't, because he'd checked. Holt rubbed Molly's neck. "Go on to bed. You'll be up to your elbows in junk in a few hours."

"Maybe you should come help," she suggested. "Get your mind off this for a little while. A break might help things come into focus better."

His focus was fine. He knew who, he just needed to prove it. And a little physical evidence to make a conviction stick. "No," he said. "You'll be safe there in public like that. Sue can stay with you and lend a hand, as well." The dispatcher had been doing a fine job the past week of keeping near Molly whenever she was likely to be alone.

"What are you going to be doing?"

"I'll be at Harriet's house again."

She stifled a yawn and padded over to the swinging door. "Coming?"

He looked at her. Her hand paused on the door, her thin yellow nightgown slipping off one shoulder.

How much time would he still have with her? A week? Maybe a few days more while she tied up the ends in Rumor before heading back to the life she'd given up in Wyoming?

"Yeah." He tossed the photo on the table and joined her.

The job could wait.

He followed her into the bedroom, and she crawled across the narrow mattress, leaving plenty of room for him. The mountain of pillows she tossed in artful disarray across the made bed every morning were now tossed over by the closet door.

He pulled off his clothes, more interested in getting skin to skin with Molly than with being tidy, and the clothes lay where they hit. He joined her, tugging her little nightgown over her head, pulling her close as he bunched the pillow under his head.

She sighed and snuggled even closer. Her knee slipped between his, and her fingertips touched the scar that ran from his knee up his thigh. "It must have been agonizing," she whispered.

He went still. It wasn't the first time she'd noticed the scar, of course. But they hadn't really talked about it. "It would have been a lot more agonizing if the machete had made it to its target. I took a lot of ribbing from Benny over the years because of it."

"He sounds like a great guy. Benny."

Holt threw an arm over his eyes. He owed his values—such as they were—to a few people. His grandfather and Benny and Joy. "If I hadn't hesitated to draw my weapon on the kid who shot him, he'd be alive."

Her hand slid over his chest, stopping over his heart. "I don't need you to tell me this, Holt. Not if you don't want to share it."

"Maybe I need to tell it." He caught her hand in his. But her fingers turned into his, and he realized she was holding on to him just as much as he was to her. "I worked gangs, I should've known better. I told you we were off duty. But down there, where we spent our days, we always wore our shields. Stayed armed. And there we were, coming out of a convenience store. Benny had a serious addiction to diet cola, and he was forever stopping at this same place. We walked out the door, and there was this kid. Big brown eyes, pretty—"

"Pretty!"

"A girl. Hanging out the window of the car that was passing on the street. I saw her, saw the colors, should have drawn, pushed Benny down, something, but she was just a girl, and—" He closed his eyes, remembering the shot, the way Benny had jerked back, the soda flying, spilling, ice hitting. "She got a clean shot on him. He never had a chance. Because I didn't draw my weapon."

"It was…a drive-by?"

"It was a hit."

"Holt—"

"I told you we'd helped take down those other officers. The gang they were protecting took care of us. We hit them. They hit back. Except the only person they hit was Benny.''

"The only person they hit with the bullet was Benny,'' Molly said quietly. "It still affected you...Benny's wife.''

"Benny's grandson. Joy and Benny, Jr. I don't know why she didn't blame me.''

"She didn't have to,'' Molly murmured. "You were probably doing it more than enough for all of you.''

Maybe. "The details got out pretty quick. I was the guy who hesitated. Nobody wanted to work with me. Hell, I didn't want to work with me. I turned in my shield.''

"And then what?''

He blew out a long breath. What did it matter if Molly knew the rest. She already knew the worst. And it wasn't as if she would be staying, once her sister came home from Africa.

"Drank myself into oblivion until Joy came around and knocked some sense into me, stuck the notice for the job here in Rumor in my hand and told me to stop shaming Benny.''

"What about the girl who fired the shot?''

"They found her. Put her in juvie. She'll probably be back on the streets in a year.''

She slid her leg over his, curling her arm around his chest. "So Rumor is your haven, too.''

He slowly stroked his hand down Molly's slender back. "Yeah. It is.''

Chapter Seventeen

"He asked me out."

Molly handed back the change for the bicycle she'd just sold and looked at Becky. "Who?"

The girl's smile could have lit a cathedral. "D.J."

"That's great."

"To the cooling-off celebration next week," Becky went on, her voice low but vibrating with excitement. "Is that the coolest?" She rolled her eyes at her unintentional pun.

"What happened with Tiffany?"

"He found her mackin' with some college guy out at Cave Springs last week."

"Mackin'?"

"Making out. You know. Same thing you do with Deputy Tanner, probably."

Molly's face flamed. She couldn't very well deny

it. The entire town knew that Holt Tanner had been living in her house ever since she'd been broken into.

"You don't seriously expect to get two dollars for this old lamp, do you?"

The voice interrupted them, and with a grin Becky headed down to the table she'd been manning with D.J.—books.

"Mr. Jupe," Molly greeted. "How nice of you to come by this morning."

"Hotter than Hades," he complained. "But at least you got awnings."

She bit the inside of her lip. "Nice of you to take off the gold fringe first before you lent them to Becky."

He made an impatient sound and plunked the lamp on the table. "This thing ain't worth more 'n fifty cents."

"But you're interested in buying it."

He tilted his head, three strands of hair and all. "Mebbe."

"I think I should have marked it fifty dollars, then," Molly said dryly. "Two dollars, Mr. Jupe. Take it or leave it."

He made a face and handed over two crumpled dollar bills. "Highway robbery," he muttered as he walked away, the lamp held carefully in his hands. Molly shook her head and reached under the table to pull out the box there to replenish her nearly bare section.

When she stood up, the sheriff was standing on the other side. "Oh!"

"Morning, Molly." He'd tucked an ugly little statue under his arm and was eating a blueberry muffin from the fragrant batch supplied by Libby Jessup. "Got yourself a nice turnout for this sale."

She exhaled a wave of nerves. "Yes. We have."

"Surprised Holt isn't with you."

"He went out to Harriet's again."

His eyebrows rose a little. "Boy works too hard," he said as he started down the row of tables.

Molly swallowed. Boy wants to keep his job, she thought. "Um, Sheriff Reingard?"

He looked back.

"I, just, um, wanted to tell you that your son has done a really fine job for us. You must be very proud of D.J."

The sheriff looked over at the young man who was working the same table as Becky. "I am. He's a good boy," he agreed. "All my kids are good." He smiled a little. "We can all thank Dee Dee for that."

"Well, I can certainly thank Dee Dee for all the items you donated." Molly waved her hand over the tables that were being pored over by half the town. "D.J. said he was killing two birds, cleaning out the garage like his mother had told him and supplying this sale at the same time."

"Yup. Cleaned a little too well, in some cases. Had to rescue this." He pulled the statue out from under his arm for a moment. "Nothing like buying back my own junk. O' course, that's what the rest of the folks here are doing, too. I've been watching people dropping off things for the sale for a month." He gave a nod and ambled on down the row, greeting people as he went.

"Hey, Dad! You gotta have this!"

Molly watched as D.J. waved something in the air,

getting the sheriff's attention. The man walked over and took the book.

The yearbook, she realized, watching the sheriff dig in his pockets and hand over some money to his son before heading away from the tables. Mrs. English was right. People did love to go through old yearbooks. He probably wanted to hide it away before too many people remembered his name was Hiram—

"Sue." Molly turned around, looking for the older woman. "Sue, I've got to go. Can you, um, supervise for me, here? I can't leave the kids alone with all this money." She pushed the cash box into Sue's hands.

"What's the matter?"

"Nothing. I'm just—just going to go call Holt."

Sue shrugged. "Okay."

But Molly was already running toward the library. She had to go around to the front, but she realized the sheriff was still out there, climbing into his patrol car now, casting a wave at someone who called out a greeting to him.

She shrank back and turned around again, running through the park, cutting across to her house. She fumbled her keys out of her pocket, cursing when she dropped them, forcing herself to take a calming breath, because she wasn't going to help Holt one bit at this rate. Inside the house she dialed his cell phone, but all she got was the recording of his deep voice saying to leave a message.

She pressed her hand to her stomach. "You'll just drive out there, Jolly Molly," she muttered. "Pretty simple."

Only, her car wouldn't start. Again.

She wanted to bang her head against the steering wheel. Instead she ran back to the library where Sue was collecting and doling out change. Holt trusted Sue. "I need your help," she said.

"I thought I might see you today." Holt watched Dave walk through Harriet's open door. He was sitting in one of the two matching chairs, the one with the pillow missing.

"Did you now. Why would that be?"

"Got any pistachios handy?" Holt held up the half shell he'd found on the floor near the desk leg. He'd known the sheriff would be by sooner or later. He'd left the two photos of Harriet's mantelpiece sitting on the seat in Dave's patrol car. Holt might not be able to identify what *was* missing from one photo to the next, but he knew for certain that Dave could. "You ought to be more careful, Dave. Leaving a trail like this. Might as well be breadcrumbs."

"What are you talking about?"

"When you came back," Holt said. "To clean up whatever loose end you'd left. What was it? Something on the mantel. That we both know. You surely saw the photos in your car. It was probably whatever you used to hit Harriet." Cold anger coursed through him. "Before you shot her with her own gun."

"You're nuts."

"No. You're nuts. Pistachio." He pushed out of the chair. "You came back to the house, Dave, and you forgot to take all your pistachio shells with you. It wasn't here the first time I went through the place."

Dave's face was red. "I'm the sheriff. You think

I don't have a right to enter a crime scene in my own county?''

''You didn't log it, Dave. You disturbed the scene and accidentally left the shell. What was it? Harriet being a little too stubborn about the baby she was carrying? Were you afraid she'd tell Dee Dee, was she blackmailing you—''

''No!'' Dave slammed the door. ''Harriet wasn't like—''

''What was she like, Dave?'' Holt leaned back against Harriet's desk. He pushed the desk chair aside a little, where Dave couldn't help but see the small bloodstain against the high back. ''Was she paranoid? Ornery? Weird about you parking out front where someone might see you? Was she hot in the sack—'' He jerked back when Dave's meaty fist flashed out, but he didn't go far enough to miss being clipped.

He rubbed his jaw, still keeping his position relaxed against the desk, painfully aware of the weight of the gun against the small of his back. But Dave had turned away, his head shaking.

''Harriet wasn't like that,'' he was saying. ''She was…smart. Had a mind of her own. Independent. Not like—''

''Dee Dee?''

Dave closed his hand over the mantel, his shoulders hunched. ''Dee Dee's a good woman,'' he said roughly. ''A *good* woman.''

Holt watched his boss through narrowed eyes. ''So you slept with Harriet because you admired your wife so much.''

''It was crazy. She wanted the baby! At our ages. And I couldn't—''

"Couldn't let that interfere with the all-American family you already had? What the hell kind of man are you?"

Dave turned, his face red. Angry. "Don't look so high and mighty, Holt. I know about you, what you came from. You let your partner bleed out on a street because you were too weak to shoot the perp."

"We got too close to you, too many times, didn't we? So you had to put us off the scent. Trying to scare off Tessa Madison. And Molly—what did Harriet do? Tell you just enough about Molly's past that you could almost emulate her ex-husband's actions?"

"You have no proof of that. You have no proof of anything."

"You've just admitted to being Harriet's lover. The father of her baby. You want me to believe that you didn't kill her, as well? Motive. Opportunity."

"Circumstantial," Dave countered. But he was sweating. "You have no physical evidence, and you know it."

"The thing that I can't quite figure is what she wrote on the book." Holt reached down and picked it up. He'd taken it from the evidence locker at the same time he'd called the state police. He turned it, showing the back of the novel, the dried blood, the smeared letters.

"And how you missed it in the first place. Why you didn't take it with you. You wiped your prints from the gun, you set the stage to look like suicide, hell, you cleaned the goddamned lint traps in the bathrooms until they looked like they were straight from the hardware store because you didn't want even a hair from your head to be found here. You probably had to shower here before you'd go home to Dee Dee after your little visits to Harriet. But you left the book. And you left something else on the mantel. Something you took a picture of when you had to come back and act the sheriff instead of the lover.''

''I didn't know about the book! It was in her lap when I...after...'' He tossed back his head. His eyes were rimmed with red. ''I came over to...discuss things. She wanted to break it off with me, but I...loved her.'' His voice was choked. ''She was going to ruin everything. My marriage, my kids. They'd all know, all because she wouldn't have a simple abortion. We could've gone on just the way we were, but no! We'd all have been ruined.''

''The only person who'd be ruined was you,'' Holt said flatly. ''There's not a soul in this town who'd blame your children or your wife for what *you* did. Rumor's not that kind of place, Dave. Remember? It's the place where everybody watches out for everybody. Where people *care*. Except for the sheriff, who's too busy cleaning up his mess, scaring innocent women along the way, to cover up for his crime—all because he couldn't keep his wick—'' He broke off, staring at the gun that Dave had drawn.

Dave's hand was shaking. But the gun was so close there was no way he'd miss his target.

Holt leaned against the desk, his hands at his side. ''I'll just be another body you have to explain, Dave,'' he said evenly.

''You've got the right initial,'' Dave said thickly. ''*H*. For...Holt? Good-lookin' guy, new to town. Younger than Harriet, she wouldn't have wanted it to get out that she'd gotten involved with a guy like you. One who'd already had a rich wife he couldn't keep—''

"*H* for Hiram.''

Holt swallowed an oath and barely managed not to lunge for the door where Molly stood, looking pale and shaky. "Get out of here, Molly."

"She loved you, Sheriff. It must have hurt when you read her journal, to see all that love she poured out for you on those pages.''

"Dammit, Molly, get—''

Dave had already grabbed her, hauling her into the living room, his arm tight around her neck.

Holt felt murderous. Molly's eyes closed, her hands on Dave's too-tight arm. "She felt guilty because of your wife, though," her voice was faint. "And so did you. Because you loved them both.''

Dave started crying. Hard, painful tears that tore out of his throat. "It was an accident.''

Molly nodded. "I'm sure it was.''

"I...just...went a little crazy. She told me she wasn't having an abortion and it was over between us.''

"You lost your temper.'' Molly's voice was all sympathy, all gentleness, despite his iron grip on her. "Maybe pushed her harder than you intended, just wanted to get her to understand you.''

"She cussed at me.'' The gun he held on Holt wavered wildly. "Woman cussed at me like I was... garbage, and she tried to leave...''

"But you couldn't let her go.'' A tear slid down Molly's cheek. Her eyes were locked on Holt. "So you hit her with something while you tried to figure out what to do. How to make things right.''

"If she'd just stayed there. But she wouldn't. She

tried to leave, said she was going to have that baby whether I liked it or not, and—''

''You reached in the drawer for the gun you'd given her and shot her with it.''

At Holt's voice Dave's attention came right back to him, front and center. The gun stopped wavering.

''Shut up. Just shut *up!*''

''Let her go, man. Let her go or I'm going to kill you.''

Dave laughed harshly. ''You can't even bring yourself to carry a piece, you fool, you think I'm going to fall for that?''

''Holt, don't—''

Holt uncoiled from the desk. ''I won't need a gun,'' he said flatly. ''Two hands will work just fine.''

''He's not going to hurt me, Holt!'' Molly's voice sounded choked. ''Are you, Sheriff. You don't want to hurt me any more than you wanted to hurt Harriet.''

Cursing, Dave shoved Molly away from him and turned for the door. But Sue Gerhardt stood there, and he shouted, swinging his gun around toward her.

Holt fired.

Chapter Eighteen

They'd drawn a crowd.

Even though Harriet's tidy white cottage with the green shutters was practically on the edge of town, there were people lining the street outside. All anxious to see what was going on beyond the flashing ambulance lights and the state police cars.

Holt turned away from the window and looked over where the EMTs were working on Dave. They'd started an IV and were working to stabilize him enough to be transported to Whitehorn.

"You didn't kill him." Molly slid her arm around his waist, burying her head against his neck. "You shot him in the leg."

Sue sniffed, looking angry. "I hope that's where you were aiming, otherwise, I'm getting you out to the shooting range first thing Monday morning."

Holt hooked his arm around the woman and pulled her close for a hug. "You are the perfect woman."

Angry, and still shocked at what her boss had done, she wiped her nose and pushed out of Holt's arm. "Enough lovey-dovey. But, uh, thanks for keeping him from shooting me."

Sue walked off, giving the sheriff a wide berth as she slipped out the door.

"Won't she have to make a statement?"

"Statements, statements and more statements," Holt said with a sigh. "But this one is cut-and-dried, at least." He closed his hands around Molly's head and gently tipped it back. "The next time I say to get out, you listen to me. I had the situation in hand. I don't know how the hell you got past the state boys, but—"

"I couldn't stand there and pretend he wasn't holding a gun on you!"

"Yes, you could have. Because if anything had happened to you, I'd—" He shook his head. "Dammit, Molly, you are a trial to my heart, you know that?"

She pressed her lips to his, laughing a little. Crying a little. "I love you too, Deputy."

Holt went still. "What?"

Molly swallowed and looked up at him.

He looked thunderstruck.

"Well? You do, don't you? Love me."

His brows drew together. He didn't look happy about it at all. "Yes."

"Then, um, maybe you won't go back to California, but...at least think about staying here? With me."

"Why would I go back to California?"

"For your career."

"I think I've got a career," he said. "Until there's a new election, or somebody else gets appointed, I'm it for the Rumor Sheriff Department. I thought you'd want to go back to Wyoming."

"Why?"

"Your sister. The life you led."

"My sister and I are free to be together now, even if she is in Wyoming and I'm here in Montana. We'll probably run up an astronomical phone bill, or maybe we'll have to get one of those little Web cams. The things you put on your computer? I don't have to worry ever again about Rob tracing me through e-mail, so…" She blinked and smiled. "My life is here," she said. "My job. Friends. You. Rumor's more than a haven. It's my home."

"Mine, too."

"Then maybe—" she swallowed again, twining her fingers through his "—we could make a home here in Rumor, together. I…I think we can, at least. Don't you?"

His eyes, so dark and serious, searched hers.

Molly's heart felt fit to burst right out of her chest, she loved him so much. Trusted him so much.

Needed him so much.

But maybe she'd been wrong—maybe this wasn't the way to take control of her life and keep it, by simply putting it out there. Saying what she wanted, speaking her mind—

Then the fine web of lines beside his eyes crinkled.

His lips tilted at the corner.

And her heart found wings.

Holt lifted their linked hands up and kissed her knuckles, then slowly slid his arms around her shoul-

ders, pulling her right up onto her toes, this woman
who was smart and brave and full of light. Who'd
changed his life in the span of days. He lowered his
mouth toward hers, feeling her breath almost as his
own.

"I do."

Epilogue

"Quite a cooling-off celebration, wouldn't you say?"

Molly laughed and stared up into the sky. There was thunder and lightning. "Good thing Mr. Jupe's awnings are put out in the park," she agreed. "We may just get rained on. He says you're the one who insisted he lend them for tonight."

Mrs. English patted her hair, looking satisfied. "Horton can be a decent man. When he feels so compelled." She picked up a glass of lemonade and picked her way across the grass in her high-heeled pumps toward the man in question.

"Where's Holt? I thought he'd be stuck to your side like glue still." Chelsea Dalton stood beside Molly. Her husband was standing at the "entrance" to the celebration. greeting and shaking hands alongside Nick Sullivan.

Molly sighed a little. She'd looked forward to dancing on the big, square dance floor that had been set out in the field that night. "He called. Got hung up with some problem on the highway."

"Get used to it," Chelsea murmured, smiling. "Sheriff's duties are never done."

"He's not the sheriff."

"Yet." She waved at a rugged-looking young man wearing a cowboy hat. "Colby, get on over here!"

Colby Holmes, Harriet's nephew, ambled over. His fiancée, Tessa, was with him. Her long, black hair floated on the breeze, drifting over the arm Colby kept around her, and Molly briefly wondered if her hair could ever get that long.

Tessa leaned forward. "It would if you didn't cut it every six weeks." Her gray eyes twinkled when Molly's lips parted in surprise.

"So, where's Holt?" Colby asked. "Figured he'd be all over this thing tonight."

Molly shrugged and repeated what she'd told Chelsea. "He'll be along as soon as he can, I'm sure."

Again Tessa smiled. It was the most serene smile Molly had ever seen. "He will. How are you feeling, Chelsea?"

Chelsea's hand drifted over her still-flat tummy. "As long as I don't get anywhere near tuna fish, I'm fine. Pierce tells me after dancing tonight, they've arranged some fireworks."

"Which won't be happening if that rain doesn't hold off," Colby said, casting an eye up at the clouds.

"They will," Tessa said, then smiled again when Colby laughed and told her to stop it. "It's just faith,'' she said. ''I have faith things will all work out just as they should.''

Molly nodded. ''I like that.''

Pierce approached, his meeting-and-greeting duties apparently fulfilled for the moment, and tucked his arm around his wife. ''You doing okay?''

Chelsea rolled her eyes. ''I'm *fine*. Unless you're going to start hovering again. Then we might have to talk.''

He grinned, and Molly watched him drop a kiss on his wife's lips. Pierce was a tall blue-eyed blonde, who looked perfectly handsome with his auburn-haired wife. And he didn't remind her of Rob at all.

''Holt told me the prints on that lightbulb Reingard took from your porch prove that he was the one who broke into your place.'' Pierce looked at Molly. ''I'm sorry for that. That I didn't somehow know Dave was—''

''None of us knew,'' Tessa said quietly.

''Well,'' Molly said, ''the bulb showed only one set of prints. Mine. He doctored the results of fingerprinting. Naturally, my fingerprints were there. It *was* my porch light, after all. In his report of my break-in, Holt didn't mention the bulb, only that the porch was dark. And it was still dark when Dave came by that evening after Holt called him. Dave never knew Holt had touched the bulb at all, because Holt tightened it *after* Dave left. If he hadn't monkeyed with the fingerprinting results there should have been two sets—mine and Holt's.''

''Reingard should have just left the bulb in the first place,'' Colby said. ''But for whatever reason, he didn't.''

''He panicked. Probably worried he'd left his own print or something. And I think he wanted Holt to catch him," Molly said. "I think his conscience was too burdened."

"I think you're giving the man more credit than he deserves," Pierce said flatly.

Chelsea rested her head against her husband's chest and pulled his arms around her. "The statue he hit Harriet with was sitting in his patrol car. He probably almost came unglued when he realized it had gone over to the rummage sale at the library. Colby and Louise both identified it as belonging to Harriet. It still had enough blood caught in the lining on the base to conclusively match it to her."

"Again, not very bright that it ended up in Dave's garage." Colby shook his head.

"And the actions of a man who wanted to be caught." Molly sipped her lemonade.

"Or one who thought he was above being caught," Pierce inserted.

"Well, no matter," Chelsea said. "It's over and done with and things can get back to normal. I do think it's sad that Dee Dee packed up all her kids and headed off."

"They'll be back," Tessa said.

A burst of music sounded from over near the dance floor. The band was tuning up. As one, people started migrating toward it. Molly looked toward the entrance. Still no sign of Holt.

"Come on, Miss Brewster." Becky Reed came up beside her. "Mr. Sullivan is ready to make an announcement about the bookmobile going back into service."

"I'll be along." Molly smiled, urging the girl on her way. She glanced one more time toward the entrance.

And delight went through her at the familiar sight

of Holt's SUV pulling up in the street already jammed with cars and bicycles. She swallowed the last of her lemonade, dropped the cup into a trash bin and headed over, smoothing down her dress as she went. She wondered how long it would be before the thought of seeing Holt would no longer cause a curl to wind through her stomach.

Maybe a lifetime.

Walking a little faster, she lifted her hand in a wave. Then went still when the passenger door of the SUV opened and a slender, blond-haired woman stepped out. Molly covered her mouth, tears flooding her eyes. "Christina."

Her sister ran toward her, and they flew into each other's arms, crying, laughing. "You're here, you're really here!"

"Your fiancé arranged it." Christina ran her hands down Molly's head, shaking. "Danny and I had barely landed back in Wyoming when Holt's message reached us. I climbed right back on a plane." She hugged Molly tightly. "This one's a good guy," she said thickly. "You can keep him around for a *long* time."

Molly looked over Christina's shoulder at Holt, meeting his strong, gentle gaze—thanking heaven that he'd barged into her life, no matter her protests.

She caught his hand in hers to press against her cheek, and watched his eyes crinkle. "I plan to," she said surely. They'd keep each other around.

For a lifetime.

"I plan to."

* * * * *

HARLEQUIN ROMANCE®

The rush of falling in love,

Cosmopolitan,
international settings,

Believable, feel-good stories
about today's women

The compelling thrill
of romantic excitement

It could happen to you!

EXPERIENCE
HARLEQUIN ROMANCE!

Available wherever Harlequin Books are sold.

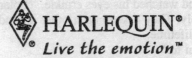

HARLEQUIN®
Live the emotion™

www.eHarlequin.com

HROMDIR04

HARLEQUIN®

AMERICAN *Romance*®

Invites *you* to experience lively, heartwarming all-American romances

Every month, we bring you four strong, sexy men, and four women who know what they want—and go all out to get it.

Enjoy stories about the pursuit of love, family and marriage in America today— *everywhere* people live and love!

AMERICAN *Romance*— **Heart, Home & Happiness**

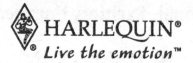

HARLEQUIN®
Live the emotion™

www.eHarlequin.com   HARDIR104

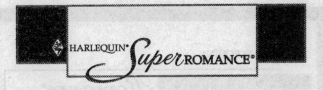

…there's more to the story!

Superromance.
A *big* satisfying read about unforgettable
characters. Each month we offer *six* very different
stories that range from family drama to adventure
and mystery, from highly emotional stories to
romantic comedies—and much more! Stories
about people you'll believe in and care about.
Stories too compelling to put down….

Our authors are among today's *best* romance
writers. You'll find familiar names and talented
newcomers. Many of them are award winners—
and you'll see why!

If you want the biggest and best
in romance fiction, you'll get it
from Superromance!

Emotional, Exciting, Unexpected…

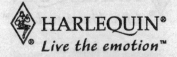

HARLEQUIN®
Live the emotion™

www.eHarlequin.com   HSDIR104

HARLEQUIN®
Presents

The world's bestselling romance series...
The series that brings you your favorite authors,
month after month:

Helen Bianchin...Emma Darcy
Lynne Graham...Penny Jordan
Miranda Lee...Sandra Marton
Anne Mather...Carole Mortimer
Susan Napier...Michelle Reid

and many more uniquely talented authors!

Wealthy, powerful, gorgeous men...
Women who have feelings just like your own...
The stories you love, set in exotic, glamorous locations...

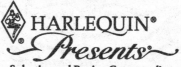

HARLEQUIN®
Presents

Seduction and Passion Guaranteed!

www.eHarlequin.com

HPDIR104

Harlequin Historicals®
Historical Romantic Adventure!

*From rugged lawmen and
valiant knights to defiant heiresses
and spirited frontierswomen,
Harlequin Historicals will
capture your imagination with
their dramatic scope, passion
and adventure.*

*Harlequin Historicals...
they're too good to miss!*

HARLEQUIN®
INTRIGUE®

WE'LL LEAVE YOU BREATHLESS!

If you've been looking for thrilling tales of contemporary passion and sensuous love stories with taut, edge-of-the-seat suspense—then you'll love Harlequin Intrigue!

Every month, you'll meet six new heroes who are guaranteed to make your spine tingle and your pulse pound. With them you'll enter into the exciting world of Harlequin Intrigue— where your life is on the line and so is your heart!

THAT'S INTRIGUE—
ROMANTIC SUSPENSE
AT ITS BEST!

HARLEQUIN®
Live the emotion™

www.eHarlequin.com   INTDIR104

V *Silhouette*

SPECIAL EDITION™

Emotional, compelling stories that capture the intensity of living, loving and creating a family in today's world.

Special Edition features bestselling authors such as Nora Roberts, Susan Mallery, Sherryl Woods, Christine Rimmer, Joan Elliott Pickart— and many more!

For a romantic, complex and emotional read, choose Silhouette Special Edition.

V *Silhouette*®

Visit Silhouette Books at www.eHarlequin.com

SSEGEN04